BAY OF FEAR

A Gothic Medieval Romance

By Kathryn Le Veque

Print Edition

Text by Kathryn Le Veque
Cover by Kim Killion

Edited by Scott Moreland

Kathryn Le Veque Novels

Medieval Romance:

De Wolfe Pack Series:
Warwolfe
The Wolfe
Nighthawk
ShadowWolfe
DarkWolfe
A Joyous de Wolfe Christmas
Serpent
A Wolfe Among Dragons
Scorpion
Dark Destroyer
The Lion of the North
Walls of Babylon

The de Russe Legacy:
The Falls of Erith
Lord of War: Black Angel
The Iron Knight
Beast
The Dark One: Dark Knight
The White Lord of Wellesbourne
Dark Moon
Dark Steel

The de Lohr Dynasty:
While Angels Slept
Rise of the Defender
Steelheart
Shadowmoor
Silversword
Spectre of the Sword
Unending Love
Archangel

Lords of East Anglia:
While Angels Slept
Godspeed

Great Lords of le Bec:
Great Protector

House of de Royans:
Lord of Winter
To the Lady Born

Lords of Eire:
Echoes of Ancient Dreams
Blacksword
The Darkland

Ancient Kings of Anglecynn:
The Whispering Night
Netherworld

Battle Lords of de Velt:
The Dark Lord
Devil's Dominion
Bay of Fear

Reign of the House of de Winter:
Lespada
Swords and Shields

De Reyne Domination:
Guardian of Darkness
With Dreams
The Fallen One

House of d'Vant:
Tender is the Knight (House of d'Vant)
The Red Fury (House of d'Vant)

The Dragonblade Series:
Fragments of Grace
Dragonblade
Island of Glass
The Savage Curtain
The Fallen One

Great Marcher Lords of de Lara
Lord of the Shadows
Dragonblade

House of St. Hever
Fragments of Grace
Island of Glass
Queen of Lost Stars

Lords of Pembury:
The Savage Curtain

Lords of Thunder: The de Shera Brotherhood Trilogy
The Thunder Lord
The Thunder Warrior
The Thunder Knight

The Great Knights of de Moray:
Shield of Kronos
The Gorgon

The House of De Nerra:
The Falls of Erith
Vestiges of Valor
Realm of Angels

Highland Warriors of Munro:
The Red Lion
Deep Into Darkness

The House of de Garr:
Lord of Light
Realm of Angels

Saxon Lords of Hage:
The Crusader
Kingdom Come

High Warriors of Rohan:
High Warrior

The House of Ashbourne:
Upon a Midnight Dream

The House of D'Aurilliac:
Valiant Chaos

The House of De Dere:
Of Love and Legend

St. John and de Gare Clans:
The Warrior Poet

The House of de Bretagne:
The Questing

The House of Summerlin:
The Legend

The Kingdom of Hendocia:
Kingdom by the Sea

Contemporary Romance:

Kathlyn Trent/Marcus Burton Series:
Valley of the Shadow
The Eden Factor
Canyon of the Sphinx

The American Heroes Anthology Series:
The Lucius Robe
Fires of Autumn
Evenshade
Sea of Dreams
Purgatory

Other non-connected Contemporary Romance:
Lady of Heaven
Darkling, I Listen
In the Dreaming Hour
River's End
The Fountain

Sons of Poseidon:
The Immortal Sea

Pirates of Britannia Series (with Eliza Knight):
Savage of the Sea by Eliza Knight
Leader of Titans by Kathryn Le Veque
The Sea Devil by Eliza Knight
Sea Wolfe by Kathryn Le Veque

Note: All Kathryn's novels are designed to be read as stand-alones, although many have cross-over characters or cross-over family groups. Novels that are grouped together have related characters or family groups. You will notice that some series have the same books; that is because they are cross-overs. A hero in one book may be the secondary character in another.

There is NO reading order except by chronology, but even in that case, you can still read the books as stand-alones. No novel is connected to another by a cliff hanger, and every book has an HEA.

Series are clearly marked. All series contain the same characters or family groups except the American Heroes Series, which is an anthology with unrelated characters.

For more information, find it in **A Reader's Guide to the Medieval World of Le Veque**.

Author's Note

Welcome to a real "dark and stormy night" novel!

I adore the Gothic genre – tragic, dark, angsty. Such fun to write and read. This isn't a traditional Gothic, where the main characters are super emotional and in constant turmoil. There is a great love story in this tale – actually, three or four of them – but there are threads of tragedy and chaos running throughout. Mostly, it's romance, but told in an unconventional way that I think you're going to love.

Our hero is Tenner de Velt. He's the grandson of not only Jax de Velt, but of Christopher de Lohr. Chris' daughter, Brielle, married Jax's son, Cassian. That pair – Cassian and Brielle – are the grandparents of Diamantha de Bretagne from "The Questing," as Diamantha's mother, Evanthe, is Tenner's elder sister. I think someday I'm going to have to write Cassian and Brielle's story since they keep appearing in family trees.

The bottom line is that Tenner is the grandson of two of the greatest knights in my Medieval world, and he's a dynamic, dedicated young knight. I really enjoyed writing about him. His lady love is Annalyla St. Lo, from the House of St. Lo, which doesn't really have a history in the World of Le Veque yet, but it will. She is sweet, and level-headed, and rather tenacious, which is fun. She's not afraid to jump in and get her hands dirty, as you'll see.

As always, a pronunciation key, since you know I like to throw weird names in the reader's direction:

Baiadepaura – BYE-uh-duh-PARR-uh (baia is "bay" in Portuguese, and "de Paura" is a family name)

Mawgwen – MAH-gwen

Annalyla – Anna-LIE-luh, or just pronounce the two names and put them together – Anna and Lyla.

Of note: There are two different spellings in this novel for de Paura – you will see it as di Paura and also as de Paura. That's because prior to the Norman Conquest, the name was spelled di Paura. It was the Normans who 'Normanized' the name and gave it a Norman spelling – *de* as opposed to *di*. Therefore, the two different spellings are not an error.

So, sit back, light a candle, and grab your talisman for a spooky trip into Medieval Cornwall where ghosts live, curses exist, and love conquers all. Just remember… sometimes things aren't always as they seem!

Enjoy!

Kathryn

Family Tree

As outlined in the novel, Tenner is the grandson of Ajax de Velt and Christopher de Lohr. There is, as of yet, no novel where Cassian de Velt and Brielle de Lohr are the hero and heroine, but that may soon change. Their children appear twice – in the novel "The Questing," and in the novel "Bay of Fear."

Children of Cassian de Velt (son of Ajax de Velt from "The Dark Lord") and Brielle de Lohr (daughter of Christopher de Lohr from "Rise of the Defender")

Evanthe (*Mother to Diamantha de Bocage from "The Questing"*)

Genica

Tenner

Blaine

Marius

Melisandra

Table of Contents

THE DEVIL OF BAIADEPAURA

(CORNISH FOLK SONG, CIRCA 14TH CENTURY)

On the cliffs of the Cornwall coast,
There lived a ghost,
A fiend with a heart of ash.

When his voice was heard,
Upon his breath, a word,
The shadow of death calls fast.

The Devil, you see,
Lived on in he,
In the stones by the raging sea.

His soul damned by the raging sea.

CHAPTER ONE

Year of Our Lord 1060
Cornwall

IT WAS A dark and stormy night.

His fortress had been under siege since yesterday, when the peasants from the nearby village charged the wood-and-iron gates with their screaming and vitriol. They weren't an army, but a mob, and with any mob, the mentality of it caused them to do things that men wouldn't normally do. They were feeding on fear, and fear made them mad. They'd come for something, something tucked back in the bowels of Baiadepaura Castle, and they were going to get it.

They'd come for him.

His home, his great castle, which had been standing for centuries, would not be enough to hold back the mob. The fortress walls were made out of piles of earth, great berms that were covered with grass, and taller than two men standing shoulder-to-feet. At the top of the walls were great pikes made from tree trunks, cut from the forests that filled the center of the country. Precious wood that was also used to build the gates, which had been soaked by the storm that had blown in from the sea, but not enough. Now, beneath the bright moon as the storm scattered, the gates were burning as the villagers built great bonfires against them.

It was only a matter of time before they collapsed.

Standing on the ground level of the keep, the lord of Baiadepaura could see the gates from where he stood, peering from a window in a chamber once used by his father to conduct business. He'd been standing here for quite some time, watching the activity, or what he could see of it. Mostly, he could smell it. Smoke was heavy in the air, mingling with the damp sea air. It was heavy and acrid, and he coughed as he breathed it in.

But it was more than the smoke that caused him to cough. The unfortunate fact was that he was sick, too, like most of the villagers, and that was why they'd come. They'd come to punish the odd, silent lord living in the old Roman ruins on the cliff as if he had somehow brought a plague to their people, a sickness that was killing them in droves. Those who weren't sick were terrified that they would be the next ones to become covered with sores, wracked with pain, before dying a hideous death.

They blamed the lord in the castle by the sea for everything.

But it wasn't his fault. Heavyset and balding, the lord coughed into a rag in his hand, one that was covered in blood from his lungs. He hadn't brought the sickness to the village; he never left the castle because he was mute and afraid of people he could not communicate with. To the villagers, however, he was a man of evil and mystery. The more he remained hidden in the fortress, the more they spoke of him in hushed tones. They feared him, and rumor had it that he could control the weather. If a storm blew in, it was because the lord was unhappy, and if fire consumed the crops or the scrub around the village, it was because the lord was cursing them.

They were terrified of the man that could not speak. Some said that if he did, he had a forked tongue and the words of the Devil would come forth.

That was how he knew the villagers were coming for him.

The Devil of Baiadepaura.

In truth, the lord didn't fear much for himself, but he did fear for his wife and child. They were in the chamber above him, both of them near death with the same sickness he had. The castle did business with the village two miles north and he had servants who would buy food from the marketplace there, but those servants were untrustworthy and cheated him constantly, knowing he couldn't verbally reprimand them or even banish them.

Being a gentle and confused soul, he wouldn't. They were servants left over from his father, a truly evil man, who had, indeed, swindled and mistreated the villagers of Treskin during his reign of terror. His father had been the real Devil of Baiadepaura. It had been the cheating, cruel servants who had brought the sickness to him from the village, but it was the sins of the father that now haunted the son named Faustus de Paura.

It was Faustus who had paid dearly for his father's evil, a man who had kept his mute son caged up like an animal for most of his early life. Only towards the end of his life, when he knew he was dying, had his father released him, telling him how stupid and freakish he was, cursing him with every breath he took. He'd even purchased a slave girl from one of the many ships that passed the coast on their way north to Eire, a slave girl who couldn't speak because her former master had cut her tongue out. His father had given him the slave girl as some manner of cruel joke, but the joke turned against him when Faustus and Anyu, the girl, had fallen in love.

A new world opened up for Faustus with the introduction of Anyu. She'd been so very sweet to him, and because she had been a concubine with duties in the days before her beauty had left her, she was able to read and write, and she taught Faustus how to write. It was how they communicated, mostly, and even now, Faustus had used the skill his wife had taught him to write a note to the villagers upon the tanned hide of a sheep, explaining that although he was sorry for their sickness, he had nothing to do with it. He begged them for their mercy.

But he suspected it would do no good.

On the floor above him, Anyu and their infant son lay dying, and the villagers who believed Faustus was responsible for the plague that swept their town were coming to kill him because of it. Faustus couldn't chance them getting their hands on Anyu and the baby. He couldn't take the chance that his wife and son would know a horrible death. Therefore, in his heart of hearts, he knew what he had to do.

As the gate began to crumble into ashes and heavy, black smoke shot up into the sky, Faustus left the sheepskin note on the table in his father's chamber, rolled up to protect the ink from smoke or water damage, and took a dagger, the only dagger he had, and made his way up to the chamber where his family was.

The thieving servants had long since fled, so there was no one to tend the sick. Faustus had been doing it himself, and as he climbed to the top of the old, creaking stairs and made his way into the chamber, he could see Anyu lying on their bed with the baby pulled up against her. As Faustus came near, he could tell simply by the look on her face that the baby was gone.

Her pale, plain face was full of sorrow and Faustus' features crumpled, but just a little; he couldn't give in to his grief, not when he had a task to complete. He loved Anyu too much to allow her to fall victim to the mob. Their perfect life was about to come to an end and he would be the one to end it. Even now, they were probably kicking away the burning gate and making their way inside the courtyard.

He had little time.

With tears streaming down his face, he smiled at his wife, who was looking up at him with utter grief, yet total trust. They couldn't speak to one another, but it didn't matter. Their expressions, their touch, said more than words ever could. Anyu reached up a blackened hand to him, with fingers rotted by the disease, and pulled him down to his knees.

Together, they wept over their son, and they kissed one another, reassuring them that their love was still strong. Nothing could take that from them. The smell of smoke was becoming heavier now, and Faustus could hear the shouts in the bailey as the villagers began their hunt for the Devil they believed responsible for their pain. There was no more time to waste.

He had to act.

With a final kiss to his wife, kissing her softly on the lips, Faustus took the dagger and rammed it into her back, between her shoulder blades, and pierced her heart. Anyu startled at the sharp pain, but the moment the blade cut into her heart, death was instant. Faustus sobbed as she collapsed over their son, embracing the child even in death. But before he could remove the dagger and turn it on himself, the door to the chamber flew open.

The room filled with angry, hostile people, and Faustus was grabbed and pulled away from Anyu and their child. The last he saw, someone was rolling her onto her back and tearing at her clothing, looking for jewels. She had none except for the necklace Faustus had given her when they were married, and that was always around her neck. As he was pulled out of the chamber by the mob, Faustus swore he saw someone yank the gold chain with the horsehead pendant off of her dead body.

That fed him with rage.

It was a rage that tore at him as he was dragged out of the keep and into the bailey, where the entire expanse of the yard had filled with angry, rioting villagers. The note he'd written was still on his father's desk, but there was no use in giving it to them now, nor could he if he'd wanted to. He was wrapped in iron chains, heavy and cutting at him, as the villagers swarmed him, hitting him with clubs and sticks and hands.

Unable to cry out, unable to scream, he took to spitting at them, weeping silently at what was happening. His only comfort was in the fact that his family was dead and unable to experience such pain and terror, but that faith was tested when he saw the villagers dragging Anyu's body from the keep and toss it onto a big fire they were making the center of the bailey.

At first, the rage in his heart multiplied as the poor woman was denied dignity in death. He opened his mouth, but no sound came forth as he rattled his chains and tried to break free. When that didn't work, he took to straining against them as if to snap them that way. The villagers, startled by such unbridled madness, stepped back, fearful that some of that madness might rub off on them. But the madness subsided, deteriorating into open-mouth weeping as Faustus looked away from the sight of his wife burning on a pyre, remembering Anyu as she had been in life and not as a corpse now going up in flames.

It was pain too deep for words, even if he could have spoken them.

With the smell of burning flesh heavy in the air, the villagers decided that a fiery grave was Faustus' destination as well. They finished hitting him and torturing him, and they dragged him over to the flames that were billowing thick, dark smoke into the twilight sky. It seemed strange to them that he went willingly, almost *too* willingly, and it was even stranger that by the time they reached the flames, the Devil of Baiadepaura didn't wait to be invited – he threw himself into the flames atop his burning wife and, without a sound or a twitch, he ignited into flames right on top of her.

For the villagers, the screaming and rioting died down and a silence of shock settled as they watched the wicked lord burn. He'd taken the pleasure away from them and thrown himself into the flames. There wasn't much satisfaction to that, they realized. In fact, there was something macabre yet poignant about it as he moved his burning body over his wife's as if to cover the woman, protecting her from the evil of the world that had killed them both.

In fact, the villagers, once so eager to execute the man, weren't so eager any longer. Now they were looking at each other with doubt, and even suspicion. Now that the object of their hate was smoldering in the ruins of the bailey, it seemed as if their hate had burned away right along with him. There was no longer anything to focus their rancor on. Even so, there was an unsettled feeling around them, as if the evil had not died with the two bodies on the flames.

The evil lingered.

Perhaps, it was their own evil they felt, hatred and ignorance so great that it had taken on a life of its own. Or perhaps, it was the fact that Faustus, in his last few moments of sanity before the pain of the fire overtook him, imagined a curse for them so great, so strong, that the pain and anguish in his soul had taken flight, escaping his burning body to hover over the castle like a storm. It touched all of them, even as they wandered away from the burning pyre, through the destroyed gates, and back to their village. The curse that had come from Faustus' very soul was one of vengeance and anger, for at the very moment his life was burned from him, he'd begged the gods of darkness for their blessing.

My vengeance upon those who killed my wife.
Against those who stole the only thing of value I'd given her.
Whoever has the necklace shall know bad fortune and sorrow.
For what they have done, let them suffer beyond suffer.
Let them know anguish until the end of time.
And let all who set foot within these walls know a bottomless, horrid fear.
I will make them pay.

Had the peasants of Treskin known of the curse Faustus had wished against them, they might have had the opportunity to ask a priest to pray for them, or seek guidance from the witches who lived in the sea caves along the coast. But they didn't know, and they returned to their lives as if they'd not just killed an innocent man.

Even so, it wasn't Faustus' curse that wiped out the village of Treskin. It was the plague that continued to kill long after the man they believed responsible was gone. Within a week, the entire village was deserted and those who hadn't become ill fled to points east, carrying the disease as they went. Several more villages in Dumnonia and even further east and north were affected by the plague that struck without warning, without prejudice to men or women or children.

In truth, Faustus never left Baiadepaura Castle. His soul, trapped by the curse, by the hatred towards those who had killed his family and had stolen his wife's necklace, the only thing of value he'd ever given her, lingered in the walls, in a dark and unsettling limbo, looking for the necklace that had been stolen from his beautiful Anyu. Waiting for the next inhabitants of Baiadepaura to unleash his anger upon.

In the castle on the cliffs, by the unforgiving and turbulent sea, the Devil of Baiadepaura waited.

CHAPTER TWO

Year of Our Lord 1268
Seven Crosses Castle, Tiverton, Devon

"I REALIZE THIS is asking a great deal of you, Tenner, but were it not important, I would not ask."

Tenner de Velt stood in the lavish solar of his lord, Ivor FitzJohn, as the man spoke of the immediate future involving Tenner and men under his command. There was displeasure in the air already, and all of it Tenner's, but he could not voice his objections to the Earl of Tiverton. The man was the child of a bastard son of King John, a cousin to the present king, and all Plantagenet if there ever was such a thing.

And what the earl wanted, the earl got.

Tenner sighed faintly.

"My lord," he said, trying to stay on an even keel. "It is my honor to carry out every command and every wish you have but, in this case, it may be better to send someone else. My betrothed, as you know, is due to arrive any day now and I am not entirely sure it is a good idea to take a woman to Baiadepaura Castle."

The unspoken reasons behind his protest hung in the air between them until Ivor broke the silence.

"Let us look at this as logical men, Tenner," he said as he moved to an elaborately carved table that held a crystal decanter of wine. The room was, if nothing else, an unashamed display of wealth of the

FitzJohn family. "My cousin, King Henry, and his brother, Richard, are at odds again. He's taken away some of Richard's properties, one of them being Baiadepaura Castle, a rather strategic outpost in Cornwall. Not that Richard ever did anything with it; he gave in to the rumors of the hauntings and curses, as you know. He felt that the place was more of a burden than an asset, but I do not view it that way. We are men of reason, Tenner; we do not believe in ghosts or curses. And Baiadepaura is strategic to the piracy that is going on all along the western coast. You know they have hit my properties in Bude and in Widemouth Bay. Baiadepaura is in a perfect position to defend these properties and now it is finally mine."

Tenner knew about the pirates devastating the earl's properties along the northern part of Cornwall's coast. That was old news, but the earl had a point – they only kept small outposts at Bude and Widemouth Bay because Henry, and his brother, Richard, wouldn't allow Tiverton to build anything resembling a castle in those lands, even if it was for the protection of Tiverton's properties.

Ivor had spent years petitioning the king to allow him to build a fortress on his properties, but Richard had convinced his brother, in a moment of alliance with him, not to allow it. Somehow, Richard, Earl of Cornwall, was afraid that his cousin, Ivor FitzJohn, might try to usurp him. No one in Cornwall could have more power than Richard, so there had been a stalemate for years until the news came that Henry would be granting FitzJohn Baiadepaura Castle.

No one wanted a cursed castle, not even greedy Richard.

But Tenner wasn't so sure it was a victory for Tiverton. Everyone in Cornwall and Devon, and beyond, knew the tales of that awful place. Ghosts and curses were only part of it. The entire area was derelict and dangerous, dotted with clumps of forests that held outlaws and murderers. Pirates were as plentiful as vermin. Because no decent folk would go into the area, it had become a haven for the worst society had to offer, so Tenner knew the ghosts of Baiadepaura weren't the only threat he would have to deal with.

It would come from everywhere.

"My lord, let me be clear," Tenner said patiently. "I do not fear ghosts, for I do not believe in such things. My primary reluctance about Baiadepaura is taking a woman there. You want me to command Baiadepaura and I am more than willing to do so; nay, I relish the challenge. But the woman I am to marry is to arrive on the morrow, I am led to believe, and I do not wish to take the woman with me to such a place. I would be unable to effectively command if I am worrying over her safety every moment of the day."

The earl was unmoved. "Then leave her here."

"I cannot, my lord."

Ivor was growing impatient, making it difficult to keep the expression off his rather unhandsome face. "De Velt, you did not want a wife at all," he said. "I was here when you received the missive from your father. Lord Cassian is a fine man and I hold no quarrel with him, but he deliberately saddled you with a wife you did not want. Is this statement untrue?"

Tenner's jaw ticked. "His decision was… unexpected."

"Do you want her?"

"Nay. But that is not my choice."

"But you would insist on taking this unwanted wife with you to Baiadepaura rather than leave her behind? That makes no sense."

Tenner lifted a dark eyebrow. "I could not shame my father by treating her poorly," he said. "Our family has a history of brutes and fiends, and I'll not add to that with the legend of a knight who wed an honorable woman and then left her behind when he went to assume a new post. My father would not believe me if I told him I left her behind for her own safety, and then he would have to explain that to her father. It would make my father look like he had a fool for a son."

FitzJohn sighed heavily. He genuinely liked Tenner; the man was as dedicated to duty as any knight he'd ever seen. The grandson of Ajax de Velt on his father's side and of Christopher de Lohr on his mother's, Tenner was a super breed of knight. He had all of Jax de Velt's size, coloring, and strength, right down to the dual-colored eyes, but all of de Lohr's wisdom, cunning, calm negotiation, and reason.

As far as knights went, Sir Tenner de Velt was as close to perfect as they came.

And Ivor knew he was very fortunate to have him. He'd actually stolen him away from the Duke of Surrey in a gambling game, and he'd cheated, because he very much wanted de Velt at the helm of his army. He'd seen how the young knight had handled Surrey's troops and he wanted the man for himself.

Years down the road, he and Surrey were no longer friends, but Tenner had been worth the cost. He and his knight got along mostly famously. Ivor had two children; an older daughter who had gone mad long ago, and an incorrigible ten-year-old son who was off to foster with de Nerra of Selbourne Castle in Hampshire. These days, Tenner was filling the role that neither of the man's children could fill, that of a child who could make a father proud. In fact, Ivor didn't like to see Tenner so unhappy but, given the circumstances, there was little choice. Ivor wanted Tenner at Baiadepaura and the knight was simply going to have to accept it.

"Then your only choice is to take the woman with you if you feel so strongly," he said, moving over to pat Tenner on his broad shoulder. "In fact, I will send de Correa and his wife with you. Your wife can have a companion in Lady de Correa, and you shall have another knight at your disposal. I will also send five hundred men with you from Seven Crosses and you have my permission to hire any artisans or laborers you need to make the castle secure and livable. And it will be *your* outpost, Tenner – you will give the commands and all men will obey you. You will be answerable only to me. All I ask is that you keep the pirates away from my properties."

Tenner resisted the urge to roll his eyes. The suggestion of an additional knight and his wife made things both better and worse. He and Arlo de Correa were great friends, and had been ever since Tenner had arrived at Seven Crosses Castle, and he sincerely had no issue with Arlo accompanying him, but the knight also came with a wife – another woman – that they would have to worry about at Baiadepaura. It was a grossly unpalatable situation.

But it was also one he couldn't refuse.

Aye, Tenner knew he couldn't refuse it and his stomach was in knots because of it.

"If you wish it, my lord," he said with reluctance. "I will do what is necessary to protect your properties in the area and your mining interests."

"And you will allow the women at Baiadepaura?"

Tenner's jaw ticked. "Against my better judgement, I will."

Ivor let out a sigh of relief. He thought he was going to have a much more difficult fight on his hands. He knew Tenner had not changed his mind about bringing a woman to Baiadepaura but, to the man's credit, he wasn't arguing about it. He was doing as his liege instructed.

The mark of a seasoned knight.

"Thank you," he finally said sincerely. "This is an important task, Tenner. I know you are aware of my production of tin mining in the area, but not the full extent because it simply hasn't been your business. You lead my armies, Tenner, not my business interests, so I've never fully informed you of the situation, but the reality of it is this – unfortunately, because of Henry and Richard, and their disallowing me to build stronger fortresses to protect my lands, the mining has been on a very small scale. There are mining towns near Bude and Widemouth Bay, where merchant ships take my tin to France and even the eastern part of England. It is those ships that the pirates target, Tenner. That much you *do* know."

Tenner nodded. "I do, my lord."

"What you do not know is that with the fortress of Baiadepaura, I can now expand the mining operations," he said. "More tin, and more wealth. All you need do is protect the ships that come in and out of the harbors by ridding the area of the pirates. That will be your task."

Tenner lifted his dark eyebrows as if to suggest that wasn't such an easy thing. “The pirates are at sea and I am on land,” he said. “Have we considered hiding soldiers on the merchant ships?”

“That is something we must discuss now that I have the freedom to protect my property more than I ever have.”

“And I fear we should have vessels ourselves to intercept the pirates who may go after the merchant ships.”

Ivor grinned. “You see?” he said as he set his wine down and turned for the table that held maps and other documents. “This will be a great challenge for your skills, Tenner. We shall discuss what you believe you might need, and I even have a rough drawing of Baiadepaura so you can see her design. It was quite difficult to come by this drawing, believe me. No one wants to go near the place, so I had to pay some of my miners to get this. In truth, I cannot guarantee the accuracy, but it is better than nothing.”

He was rummaging through his desk, a cluttered thing, and knocked over a precious inkwell in the process, which he dismissed with a wave of the hand, knowing he had a dozen such inkwells at his disposal. As the silver inkwell lay on the floor and bled dark ink onto the stone, Ivor brought a large piece of vellum over to Tenner.

As Ivor had feared, it wasn’t much to go on. Men had drawn on the vellum with ink that was fading, looking more like brown scratches in a semi-recognizable pattern, but Tenner received the impression of a castle of an odd shape, probably due to the fact that it was built up against the edge of a cliff. In fact, the keep seemed precariously close to those cliffs. He pointed at it.

“Is there no wall against the sea?” he asked. “From this drawing, it looks as if the wall does not extend along the cliffs. Are there walls only on three sides, then?”

Ivor nodded. “From what I understand, the sea is used as the fourth wall and the keep is built up against it.” He turned the drawing sideways to try and gain another perspective. “I am told by the miners that Baiadepaura was built on an ancient Roman fortress and that some of the walls are left there from the Romans. Surely something that has stood for so long must be strong. And the Romans were great military tacticians so, mayhap, they believed they did not need a wall along the cliff's edge."

Tenner thought it all looked rather unsafe and unsecure. "I suppose I shall find out soon enough," he said. "May I take this vellum with me? I should like to study it."

Ivor handed it to him. "Of course," he said. "And, Tenner… I should like for you to leave as soon as you marry your betrothed, so be prepared to leave immediately. Do not let the lady get settled in."

Tenner eyed him. "She is coming from Northumbria, my lord," he said. "She is not even allowed to rest before we head to the western coast?"

Ivor shook his head firmly. "Nay," he said. "Her trunks will be packed when she arrives, so she will be ready to continue on. Her stop at Seven Crosses will be for the wedding and nothing more. She will assume her wifely duties alongside you at Baiadepaura."

Tenner thought that was rather cruel, but he didn't comment. Women were weak creatures and he was of the school that they should be respected and treated with care, but Ivor wasn't of that same mindset.

It was all business as far as FitzJohn was concerned, and nothing would stand in his way.

Excusing himself from his lord's solar, Tenner headed out of the tall, square-shaped keep and into the night beyond. It was a damp night, and cold, with a fog rolling in from the sea and settling heavily upon the moors. He could smell the salt in the air and feel the dampness on his skin.

Overhead, the fog wasn't quite thick enough yet to obscure the moon and he glanced up, seeing the streaks over the moon, creating a wraith-like image.

Ghosts.

Baiadepaura Castle was famous for them. Everyone in Cornwall and western Devon had heard of the haunting of Baiadepaura, how the specter of an evil lord roamed the grounds, looking for the gold he'd buried in the walls. At least, that was the rumor. Some said there was also a lady dressed in a pale gown who wandered the battlements, only to be seen on moonless nights. Legend said that if a man saw the lady in white, his death would follow shortly.

All sorts of rumors swirled around Baiadepaura, which Ivor had readily discounted. That was easy for him to do, considering he wasn't going to be there. Truthfully, Tenner wasn't sure he believed in any of that. He was a man of reason. But he wasn't so sure of things that he didn't have some doubt. Where there was smoke, there was fire…

And where there were legends, there was quite possibly some truth to them.

Unfortunately, Tenner was about to find out.

CHAPTER THREE

THE MORNING WAS completely blanketed in white.

Emerging from the old tavern she'd spent the night in, a woman wrapped in dark green wool paused just outside the door, seeing that the land around her was, literally, white. The sun was up, so there was some illumination to the mist, but she'd never seen such fog in her entire life.

"Lady Annalyla!"

Someone was calling her name, but she couldn't see who it was. There could have been an army of cutthroats out there for all she knew and, being blinded by the white, she could very well walk right into them. So much for her first trip away from home and her hopes on finding a pleasant marriage. Her husband would be a widower before she even arrived.

Blasted fog!

"My lady, over here!"

Blinking, trying to orient her vision, she saw movement over to her left. Coming through the fog was the commander of her escort, her father's only knight, who had led her and the St. Lo contingent all the way from Roseden Castle in Northumberland to Devon. That was where they were now. It had already taken them seventeen days to reach this point, and Lady Annalyla St. Lo was coming to think they would never reach their destination. Her entire life seemed to be consumed with travel, that monotonous existence of endlessly rutted roads, mud, and foul weather. But it was all quite necessary to reach the prize at the end of the journey.

The prize of a prestigious young knight from a wealthy family.

"Good morn, Graham," she said to the knight, an older man with pocked skin. "How close are we to Seven Crosses?"

Sir Graham de Lave pointed a finger off into the fog. "We should be there by the nooning hour, my lady," he said. "If this fog would lift, you could see the country this far south. It is quite pleasant to behold."

She pulled her expensive woolen cloak tighter around her, the cloak that had taken the last of her family's ready fortune to purchase.

"Hopefully, I shall see it at some point," she said. "Is Mother Angel in the carriage?"

Graham nodded. "Aye, my lady."

He reached out to take her by the elbow and help her navigate the muddy road. The heavily-fortified carriage was there, the one that the de Velt family had loaned them for the trip, considering Annalyla was marrying the eldest de Velt son. It was a fine thing with iron and wooden sides and roof, and cushioned benches inside big enough to lay down upon. Annalyla had done just that, many times, on the never-ending journey south.

Reaching the carriage, Graham opened the door and nearly lifted her inside, helping her keep her skirts and cloak out of the mud. As Annalyla entered, a woman's thin voice filled the air.

"Sit down, child," she said crisply. "Sit down and read your scripture book. You will need the verses to fortify you before you meet your future husband. You must be prepared, child."

Annalyla eyed the woman as the door to the carriage was shut and secured, and the carriage lurched as the men began to move. Annalyla yelped as she lost her balance and tumbled onto one of the cushioned benches.

"Prepared for what?" she said as she straightened up on the bench. "Marriage? I have been prepared for that for the past year, ever since this contract was brokered. I know my role in this, Mother Angel. You need not tell me yet again what I already know."

Mother Angel had been Annalyla's nurse since she'd been an infant, brought from the House of de Vesci because Annalyla's mother could not tend the infant. A weak woman, and ashamed the child she bore was a girl, Lady Lyla de Gare St. Lo had retreated into a haze of alcohol and self-pity while her husband brought in a suitable nurse to keep the child alive.

Therefore, Mother Angel truly looked at herself as Annalyla's mother, meaning she was strict when she needed to be, but never loving. Always firm, always in control. Like now: Annalyla had to understand her role in this situation and Mother Angel had to ensure her manner was appropriately domineering.

"Your father has schooled you on your position," Mother Angel said, her beady-eyed gaze fixed upon her charge. "He has schooled me as well. I understand your role in this marriage better than you do, so take heed before we arrive. There will be no room for doubt or mistakes."

Annalyla sighed heavily. "I know that I am to be an attentive, courteous wife."

Mother Angel made a hissing sound between her teeth. "It is more than that," she said. Then, she lowered her voice. "The money is gone, child. The St. Lo money has long been gone and all we have now is our good name, a name that your father was able to rely upon to secure this marital contract. It will save your family."

Annalyla knew this; she'd known it for years. The House of St. Lo had been wealthy, once, but no longer. Blight and wars had drained their coffers, and her father had never been very good with money. He was a kind man, well-liked, but a fool when it came to coin. They still had the lands, and the properties, so Cain St. Lo had used that to his advantage when seeking a rich family for his only child to marry into.

The House of de Velt was a neighbor, and an ally, and Cain had convinced Cassian de Velt that Annalyla would be a perfect match for

Tenner, his eldest son. Through Annalyla, Tenner would inherit the St. Lo properties, but the land was all there was. There was nothing else. Cain had spent his last few coins on a suitable wardrobe for his child and an offering of a beautiful sword to give to her new husband but, after that, there was nothing left.

Tenner de Velt wouldn't know until it was too late.

"I have told my father and I shall tell you," Annalyla said with some frustration. "I will not steal from my husband and send money to Roseden. I will not enter into this marriage as a thief."

Mother Angel cast her a sharp glare. "No one has asked you to steal," she said. "But if your father needs money, and asks for it, it is your duty to obtain it from your husband."

Annalyla sat back against the cab, turning to look from the window slit at the fog that still covered the land.

"It seems so deceitful," she muttered. "I am carrying a lie into this marriage."

"You are doing what is necessary for your family to survive. There is no shame in that."

Annalyla didn't reply. Mother Angel saw it one way, and she saw it another. She didn't look at the woman, refusing to comment on a conversation they'd had far too many times. Instead, she gazed out of the window until she saw movement from the corner of her eye, daring to glance over to see that Mother Angel had collected her sewing. She was continuing work on the same piece she'd been working on the entire journey. It was an intricately flowered piece, meant to be a panel on a fine dress that Annalyla would have made someday.

A garment her new husband would pay for.

In truth, there had been some disagreement over the true purpose of this marriage. A business arrangement had turned into the method of survival just as Mother Angel had said. Annalyla had always hoped to marry a man she could be fond of, and someone who could be fond of her, but she already felt deceitful going into this marriage with de Velt and, sooner or later, the truth would be known. She greatly feared that her husband would resent her after that, and she didn't want to live the rest of her life with a man who resented her.

Unfortunately, there was nothing Annalyla could do about it. All she could do was try to protect the dark secret her family held and hope that when her husband did find out about it, it would be well into the marriage and he would consider her more valuable than the destitute house he would inherit.

That was the hope, anyway.

The carriage bumped and rolled over miles of road that had seen a great deal of travel. Mostly, they ended up in the ruts, which would grind against the axles and vibrate the entire carriage but, gradually, the road evened out and the fog began to lift. Annalyla found herself looking at green flatlands with scrub, and the road itself was made of red earth. It was red dirt as far as the eye could see. Though the land seemed to have little by way of hills or other landmarks, she could see a large forest to the north. She caught sight of Graham riding next to the carriage.

"Graham?" she asked. "You've not spoken much about our destination, but do you know anything about these lands?"

Graham was in full battle armor. He had the look of a hunter about him, a nervous energy to his movements.

"We are heading to the Gates of Hades, my lady," he said, rather ominously. "Though these lands are pleasing to the eye, they have a sinister soul."

Annalyla looked at him, though it was only through the slit in the cab wall. All he could see were her eyes. "I have heard that Devon and Cornwall are wild and uncivilized," she said. "My father told me that my betrothed came down to the south to help tame the area."

Graham grunted. "A de Velt can tame anything," he said. "But I am not sure even a de Velt knight can bring this terrible place under control."

Annalyla began to notice just how nervous he appeared. "You are afraid?"

He shook his head. "Not afraid," he said. "Prepared. The forests of Cornwall and Devon hide the barbarians. I wish your father had sent me with more men."

"He did not have any more to spare."

"Then he should have asked de Velt for more men."

"He asked for the carriage. He did not wish to ask for more."

Graham knew that. He'd served St. Lo since before Annalyla was born, a kind but rather dense man. Graham was more family than servant, and even though he knew the House of St. Lo was destitute and could hardly afford a knight of his caliber, still, he remained. Roseden was his home, after all, and his three sons had been born there, men who had moved off to bigger and more lucrative posts. Graham's wife had died two years ago, and he simply couldn't bring himself to leave the place where she was buried. Perhaps that was a foolish inclination, but Graham's loyalty was strong to the House of St. Lo, for better or for worse.

These days, it was for worse, and he had the same sense of underhandedness in this situation that Annalyla did.

He didn't think betraying the trust of a de Velt was a good idea.

"For your safety, he should have asked for more men," he said after a moment, turning to look at the untamed lands surrounding them. "My father's family came from Cornwall, and many a time in my youth did I spend time there with my grandfather."

"Is that so?" Annalyla said. "You did not mention that."

Graham nodded as if suddenly reliving old memories. "My grandfather had been a great knight, once, but an injury crippled him and he became a fisherman to feed his family," he said. "A greater man I've never seen. He could do anything."

Annalyla was listening intently. "Why have you never told me this before?"

He shrugged. "I suppose it never came up," he said. "Your father knows, however. Mayhap, that is why he did not ask de Velt for more men for the escort. I am sure he believed I could handle whatever came along, given that part of my family is from the area. But the last time I was here was a very long time ago. There are more tales and legends of these parts than anywhere else in England."

She was interested. "Like what?"

Graham's gaze was towards the north, where there was a dark line of trees in the distance. "This is a land of fairies," he said. "Piskies, they're called. You'll see the entrance to their homes in mounds or stone circles. They are playful, but they have a wicked side as well. 'Tis best to stay away from them."

Annalyla was enthralled. "Piskies," she repeated. "Have you ever seen any?"

He nodded with confidence. "Many times," he said. "But I never went near them. You should not, either."

Annalyla tried to picture wicked but playful fairies in her mind. "I will not," she promised. "What else?"

Graham could see that he had a captive audience and it amused him. "Giants," he said. "Cornwall is a land of giants, though I've not seen any myself. Some say they died out long ago. And then there is good King Arthur, of course. He lived in Cornwall."

"I have heard of King Arthur," Annalyla said. "He and his knights searched for the Holy Grail, did they not?"

Graham nodded. "They did," he replied. "His castle, Tintagel, is reputed to be haunted, but Tintagel is just one haunted castle in a land that is full of them. It seems that every town has a legend of a haunted fortress or castle, especially on the western coast."

"Is that where your grandfather lived?" Annalyla asked. "Along the western coast?"

Graham looked at her. "In fact, he did," he said. "He took up fishing out of a village in Devon, right along the Cornwall border. It was a little fishing village called Duckpool. Some of my fondest memories are from my youth, sailing the coast of Cornwall and seeing the cliffs and the rocks, listening to my grandfather tell stories of the land."

Annalyla smiled faintly, seeing the pleasant memories reflecting on

Graham's features. "He told you of the giants and the haunted castles?"

Graham nodded. "And of the mermaids who climb onto the rocks and lure fishermen to their doom," he said. "If you ever hear a woman's voice calling from the sea, do not investigate. They want your soul."

That sounded frightening and Annalyla's eyes widened. "Is it true?"

Graham fought off a grin. "Some say it is," he said. "But more importantly, there are certain castles you do not want to have anything to do with. If you are to live in this area of Devon and Cornwall, then you should know not to go to Tintagel. The placed is cursed."

"But what if my husband wishes to take me there?"

"He will not. I am sure he knows better. Another place to avoid is Blagg Castle. It is said that trolls live in the castle well, waiting for unsuspecting men to come by so that they may eat them."

Her mouth popped open. "*Eat* them?" she said with disgust. "That cannot be true. Did your grandfather tell you that?"

He lifted an eyebrow at her. "Are you calling my grandfather a liar?"

Annalyla backed down. "Well," she said slowly, "I am not, I suppose. But it sounds awful. Are there any other terrible places?"

"Baiadepaura Castle."

She looked at him curiously, repeating the oddly-named castle. "Baiadepaura? Where is that one?"

Graham lifted a finger towards the west, straight ahead. "Not far from Tintagel," he said. "It is a few miles up the coast, near a town called Bude. If ever there was a cursed place, it is Baiadepaura."

Annalyla was very interested. "Why?"

Graham pursed his lips thoughtfully. "It has a long legacy," he said. "My grandfather told me that the castle is built on the foundations of an old Roman temple, one used to worship Poseidon, the sea god. The temple was sacked when the Romans left Britain, but a local lord built his castle there and the family, the de Paura family, had a terrible legacy there."

"Why was it terrible?"

"Because the last lord was burned alive for bringing a plague to the area and legend says he still walks the ruins, looking to wreak havoc on anyone that comes near." Graham could see she was hanging on every word. "Much like the mermaids, if you hear a voice luring you into Baiadepaura, do not answer. It is the Devil of Baiadepaura luring you to your death."

"The Devil!" she gasped.

"So the legends say."

Annalyla's eyes glittered as she thought on the curse of a castle built upon Roman ruins. "Baiadepaura," she repeated. "The last part of the name is the family name, but what does it all mean?"

Graham was looking off towards the west as if to see that terrible place from the cobwebs of his memory. "It means Bay of de Paura," he said. "The family was not from Cornwall, but from Portugal, so the bay that the castle sits on was known as the Bay of de Paura. That's how the castle got its name over the centuries, in fact – it became Baiadepaura. But the bay has another name, too."

"What's that?"

"Bay of Fear."

It was a delightfully scary story, one Annalyla found quite fascinating. When Graham winked at her as if to let her know to take the stories with a grain of salt, she grinned, thinking his tales to be quite thrilling.

"Rubbish," Mother Angel suddenly hissed.

The old woman's rasp broke the spell. Annalyla turned to the woman as she sat against the wall of the cab, stitching her careful stitches.

"And how would you know that?" she asked. "Graham lived here as a child. Are *you* calling his grandfather a liar?"

Mother Angel ignored her, instead, directing her barbs at Graham. "Keep your foolish tales to yourself," she scolded. "This child has enough to worry over without you filling her head full of nonsense."

Graham simply bowed his head gallantly and spurred his horse forward and away from the carriage. He didn't much like Mother

Angel; he never had. She was an old bitch who tried to exercise her power over everyone, including a spirited young woman. When Annalyla saw that there would be no more stories, she growled with frustration and plopped back onto the bench.

"What does it matter if the stories are not true?" she demanded. "Let the man entertain me, for God's sake. I've spent seventeen days on the road with you and I can no longer stand the sight of you!"

Mother Angel didn't rise to the insult. She kept stitching. "Sit down and resume your reading," she said. "You were on the Book of Job, I believe."

Annalyla looked at the Bible sitting on the bench next to her. "I *feel* like the Book of Job," she muttered.

"What did you say?"

"I said I do not feel like reading the Book of Job."

"Then sit quietly and meditate. Think on your betrothed and how you intend to greet him."

Annalyla lay back on the bench, kicking her feet up on the walls in a petulant gesture. "I do not need to meditate on that," she said. "I shall tell him how honored I am to finally meet him, and how honored and proud I am to marry into the House of de Velt."

"And what else?"

"That he should feed you to the dogs."

Mother Angel missed her stitch, instead, sending the bone needle right over into Annalyla's foot, which was near her head. She made contact and immediately drew blood. The young woman yelped, sitting up quickly to rub the offended foot.

"Ouch!" she said, hand on her foot. "That was unnecessary!"

Mother Angel calmly returned to her sewing as if she'd not just stabbed someone. "Annie, I know you are weary, but your lack of manners and respect are uncalled for," she said. "Now, tell me – what else shall you tell your future husband? We have practiced this. Tell me all of it."

Unless she wanted to risk another stab by the needle, Annalyla was inclined to do as she was asked. According to Graham, they would be at Seven Crosses Castle before the nooning meal, meaning it would only be a matter of a few hours at most. Considering her father and Mother Angel had forced her to memorize an entire speech, Annalyla thought she'd better practice it a little so she didn't look like a fool in front of the man. She wanted to look polished and practiced, and like someone he might be proud to be married to.

God help her, she prayed it would go well.

Soon enough, she would know.

CHAPTER FOUR

Seven Crosses Castle

"Her carriage is coming through the village," Arlo de Correa gave his smart report to Tenner. "Not a very big escort party, I must say. I expected hundreds of men at the very least."

Tenner was standing in the mud-strewn bailey of Seven Crosses, having been summoned from the great hall, where he'd been studying the map of Baiadepaura that Ivor had given him. He wasn't shaved, or washed, and he was wearing clothes that he'd had on for three days. With Arlo's news, he rubbed at his chin in an indecisive gesture.

"How far away would you say she is?" he asked.

Arlo knew how reluctant Tenner had been for this marriage. He could hear the tone in Tenner's voice, like a man about to be taken to the gallows. In truth, he'd done everything possible to encourage Tenner about it, but the man would not be soothed. Arlo found some humor in that.

"Less than a half-hour, I should think," he said. "You have time to shave if you do it quickly. In case you don't know, women like their men to be clean shaven."

Tenner made a face at the man. "No one asked you."

"I know you did not, but I am telling you. And the longer you stand here, the less time you'll have to clean yourself up. Honestly, Ten, you smell like a compost heap. Men don't care, but women will."

Tenner sighed sharply, eyeing the knight that was about five years older than he was. Arlo was his closest friend, a big man with dark hair and eyes that crinkled when he smiled. He was pleasant and intelligent, with a distinct sense of command. He'd been Ivor's captain until Tenner had been brought to Seven Crosses but, much to Arlo's credit, he never made Tenner feel unwelcome or unwanted, even though he found himself playing second to the new knight. He'd done everything in his power to make Tenner feel comfortable in his new command, and it was a kindness Tenner would never forget.

Arlo was one of the good ones.

"And what if I do not want to clean up?" Tenner hissed. "There is no use in giving her a false impression. I do not plan to clean up for her every day. She may as well get used to me as I am."

Arlo was genuinely trying not to laugh. "Ten," he said, lowering his voice. "You are to be married today. I have sent to town for the priest already, and the man should arrive around the time your betrothed does. Do you truly intend to be married with uncombed hair and a growth of beard? You look like a man who lives in a cave and hates the sight of civilization. If you do not shave, my wife will rush at you with a razor and demand I hold you down. I will have no choice but to listen to her. Would you truly put me in that position?"

Tenner snarled as he fought for a retort, but one wouldn't come to mind quickly enough. Besides… he knew Arlo was correct. He just didn't want to admit it.

"She is not going to like the sight of me as it is," he finally mumbled. "No woman does."

Arlo frowned. "Are you mad? Every woman that sees you goes insane for your luxurious hair and dimpled cheeks. If you smelled better, you'd have the whole of female England after you."

Tenner shook his head, making a motion with his hand around his eyes. "Only until they see these."

Arlo knew what he meant; Tenner had inherited the de Velt trait of the two-colored eyes that most of his male line carried. The eyes were brown for the most part, but there was always a streak of green in one of them. Tenner's grandfather, Jax de Velt, had been famous for his "devil eyes" because one eye had a huge splash of bright green in it, giving the man a rather sinister appearance. Tenner's father, Cassian, who had been his father's youngest son, had inherited his mother's eyes and had been spared the brown and green combination, but Tenner had the pronounced trait, as did his brother, Marius, and his youngest sister, Melisandra. Three of the seven siblings had that distinct trait.

In Tenner's case, the green wasn't a splash so much as it was a streak right through his right eye. It was as if someone took a paint brush and slashed it across the iris at an angle, from top to bottom. Arlo didn't think it was too pronounced, but it was evident, and Tenner was self-conscious about it. He used it as a weapon at times, glaring at men who feared his two-colored de Velt eyes. But when it came to women, he'd always let part of his long hair hang in his face, covering up the right eye, so all they saw was the left mono-colored brown eye.

"I am sure she will not care," Arlo said after a moment. "She'll be much more put-off by the fact that you smell like a barnyard. For God's sake, Ten, go and wash yourself and shave. Do it before I am forced to call forth my wife."

"I am not afraid of her."

"If you are sincere, I will call her forth and see just how much of a stand you take against her when she tells you that you smell like a pig."

Tenner wasn't apt to put up a fight against Arlo's wife, Maude, a woman he genuinely liked, but a lady who was as bold as a harpy. She was loud and bold, but generous and humorous. He always had a good laugh with her. But in this case, it was no laughing matter and he had little choice if Maude took hold of him. With another sharp sigh, he turned for the knight's quarters, built into the wall of the outer bailey, and took off at a dead run.

He swore he could hear Arlo laughing behind him.

Once inside the dim chamber he called his own, with its messy bed and cluttered floor, he hunted down fresh water and took a bar of soap he rarely used, lathering it all up and very carefully shaving with his sharp razor. He didn't have hot water, but he didn't want to wait for it, so he was forced to shave with the cold and did a moderately good job of it in just a few minutes.

Stripping down to his breeches, he used some of the soap and cold water to wash his neck and chest, now paranoid that he really did smell like a barnyard and, deep down, not wanting to. Nay, he didn't want his betrothed thinking he smelled like a pig, so he quickly remedied that and went in search of his comb and a clean tunic, but finding either in his mess of a chamber was like hunting for a needle in a haystack. He finally found a reasonably clean tunic, but not his comb, so he simply wetted his hair and ran his fingers through it, hoping that would be enough.

Since his window faced out onto the bailey, he could hear when the sentries put up the call because the St. Lo escort had arrived. Rushing to the window, he peered outside, seeing that the gates were open. He could also see Arlo standing near the gatehouse and he was certain that somewhere inside the keep, Ivor had heard the cries and that he, too, was heading out to greet the soon-to-be Lady de Velt.

Stepping away from the window, Tenner ran his fingers through his shoulder-length hair one last time before heading out into the bailey, moving towards the gatehouse as the first of the escort began to enter. He could see heavily-armed men-at-arms and at least one knight, followed by a fortified carriage. He knew his betrothed was inside the carriage and he wondered if she could see him already.

That made him nervous.

With that thought, Tenner did what he usually did when facing a woman – he tucked his long hair behind his left ear while allowing the hair on the right side to drape over his right eye. He spent a good deal of his life like that, hiding his right eye. But in this case, he did it to preserve the lady's feelings. He had no idea what she looked like; all he knew was that *he* didn't want to look like a demon to her. *Devil's eyes.* His grandfather had heard that curse, as had Tenner when he'd been younger. When he'd fostered, the boys around him used to tease him about it.

He didn't want the lady thinking the same thing.

As the carriage rolled to a halt, he headed towards it.

It was time to meet the wife he didn't want.

SHE SAW HIM coming from the window.

Annalyla happened to be looking at the bailey of Seven Crosses Castle, a vast thing that was crowded with men and animals, but her attention happened to fall on a man emerging from a moss-covered stone outbuilding that was built against the fortress walls. She noticed him purely because he was wearing only a pale tunic that seemed oddly out of place among so many men wearing armor and mail and weapons. He wasn't wearing anything at all other than the tunic, leather breeches, and boots that came up past his knees.

But as the carriage came to a halt and he drew nearer, she mostly watched him because he was handsome. She'd never seen anyone like him. He had hair to his shoulders, dark like a raven's wing, and his face was partially obscured by it, but she could see enough to know that he had a square jaw and even features. He was also very tall, and very big, and she could see the size of his arms as they strained against that white tunic.

Her heart fluttered at the sight, but she tore her gaze away from him, feeling strangely disappointed that she couldn't marry a man like that. She was certain her husband was one of those clad in armor, with big weapons, a career knight from a family full of them. She braced herself for the man she thought he was – probably cold, probably unhappy he now had a wife to think of, and all of that hadn't really bothered her until this very moment. Perhaps she'd been putting off facing the truth, an entire year of being resigned to the inevitable, but now she realized that she was quite nervous about it.

The cold, unhappy husband who was about to marry into a destitute family.

"Smooth your hair, Annie," Mother Angel hissed at her. "You look unkempt."

Those words didn't help her nerves. Annalyla began smoothing at her hair, hoping to look presentable. Clad in the green wool, at least she looked the part. She looked like an heiress even if it was far from the truth. Mother Angel came to sit on the bench next to her, also smoothing at her hair, which was pulled into a large braid, with other smaller braids around her face, all of them pulled back into an intricate braid at the back of her head. It was an attractive style, or so she thought, and Mother Angel even pinched her cheeks to bring some color into them. She was just slapping the woman's hands away when the door to the carriage lurched open and a body stood in the opening.

"Come, Lady Annalyla," Graham said quietly. "We have arrived."

His hand extended into the carriage and she took it. Carefully, he helped her out into the sunshine, which had become quite bright now that the fog had burned away. Blinking her eyes in the bright light, she was immediately set upon by an older man with a droopy eyelid and dirty, faded hair.

"My lady," he said. "I am Ivor FitzJohn, the Earl of Tiverton. Welcome to Seven Crosses Castle."

Annalyla blinked at the man, squinting in the sunlight. "My lord," she said, dipping into a practiced curtsy. "It is an honor to meet you. I am Annalyla St. Lo, and this is my nurse, Mother Angel."

She indicated the older woman with the severe wimple as the woman climbed out of the carriage, but Ivor had no interest in a nurse. His focus was on the angelic-looking young woman.

"I trust you had a pleasant trip, my lady?" Ivor asked.

Annalyla nodded. "I have never been south of York, so it was a wondrous journey," she said. "I am happy to be here, my lord."

"And you are, no doubt, anxious to meet your betrothed."

"Of course, my lord."

Ivor grinned, turning to look for Tenner, who was just coming around the front of the matched pair pulling the carriage. "Ah," he said. "Here is the man you have been waiting to meet. Sir Tenner de Velt, meet your betrothed, Lady Annalyla St. Lo."

Ivor made the introduction with a good deal of relish, as if he were far too delighted in the beauty of Tenner's betrothed and dying to see the knight's reaction to it. But Tenner didn't give him the satisfaction. He looked at the young woman without emotion and gallantly dipped his head.

"My lady," he said. "I am honored."

As Ivor was disappointed in Tenner's lack of reaction to such a lovely woman, Annalyla's reaction to Tenner was just the opposite.

So the man in the pale tunic is my betrothed!

Annalyla could hardly believe her eyes. She stared at him for a moment, probably for too long, before finally lowering herself into a polite curtsy.

"My lord," she said. "The honor is mine. May I say how truly humbled my family is to unite with the great House of de Velt, and my father sends his personal greeting to you."

By the time Annalyla came up to look him in the face again, she realized that her knees were quivering. In fact, everything seemed like it was quivering, made worse when she looked into his face to see just how truly handsome he was.

It was like a dream.

Lord, she hadn't been expecting this. Not in a million years and, suddenly, all of the deceit she'd brought with her was weighing down upon her like a boulder, pressing down until she could hardly breathe. This handsome knight, who could probably have had any woman in England with his looks and breeding, was entering into a marriage with a woman who brought absolutely nothing with her. Technically, she was the heiress to the House of St. Lo, but it was an empty title. Only Tenner didn't know it.

She was starting to feel sick to her stomach.

"I've not met your father, but my father thinks highly of him," Tenner said, cutting into her thoughts. "Believe me, he is quite happy about this. I think it would be a contest to discover whose father was the most joyful."

His eye, the one she could see, was twinkling with mirth, and she grinned, feeling her heart turn giddy. It was quivering just like the rest of her, so much so that she was very nearly startled when Tenner suddenly extended a hand to her.

"If you will come with me, we shall retreat inside the hall," he said. "I should not like to have our first conversation out here in the open for all to hear. Will you come?"

Annalyla nodded eagerly, *too* eagerly, and took his extended hand. He smiled at her, just a little, and she swore she was about to faint. She hoped she wasn't coming across like a foolish young maiden, but the truth was that she was caught completely off-guard by the sheer beauty and magnetism of her future husband. She kept expecting someone to tell her that it was all a joke, and that her real uncomely and lazy husband was waiting for her in the great hall, which was where they were headed. But no great laughter or jesting came forth, from anyone. It seemed that the knight who had tucked her hand into the crook of his elbow really *was* Tenner de Velt. God help her, it was all true.

It was both the happiest and most distressing day of her life.

THANK GOD HE'D shaved. And washed.

Thank God for small mercies!

Tenner felt like he was in a daze. He had an angel on his arm and he'd never been more aware of anything in his entire life.

This is the woman I am to marry?

He had to force himself not to look at her as they headed into the great hall of Seven Crosses, but he kept rolling the memory of her over and over in his mind – she was fair, with long, blonde hair and skin like cream. Her eyes were big and bright, a pale shade of green with a dark ring around the irises. He noticed that kind of thing about other people's eyes, and he noticed it about hers. With her pert nose and perfect lips, he was starting to feel like a fool.

An undeserving fool.

But he kept his composure as he took her into the great hall. He knew that Maude, Arlo's wife, had arranged for refreshments, so the moment he entered with the petite lady on his arm, the servants began to scatter. People were filtering into the great hall and, very quickly, pitchers of wine and cups were brought forth.

Tenner took Annalyla to a table near the hearth and barked at a servant to stoke the fire, as the day was rather cool. As he helped her to sit, politely removing her heavy woolen cloak with the fur lining, Ivor planted himself right next to her and started a conversation.

"Tell us of your delightful trip from Northumberland," he said. "Were you on the road a long time?"

Annalyla glanced over at Graham, who was sitting down at the table next to her, along with Mother Angel. She didn't want to give the wrong answer to anything, and was looking to Graham and Mother Angel for support, but they were too far away to hear what was being said. Annalyla answered, hoping she wouldn't make a fool of herself.

"This is our seventeenth day, my lord," she said. "We were very fortunate to have good weather most of the time, except in the north. It rained steadily until we reached Sheffield. After that, our days were mostly clear."

Ivor nodded, handing the lady the cup of wine that a servant placed before him. "Drink," he said. "You must be quite weary after all of the travel you have endured. Do you have any interesting stories to tell? Anything that happened to you as you journeyed south?"

Annalyla sipped at the tart wine. "Nothing of note, my lord," she said. "We did not suffer any danger, thankfully."

Ivor had hoped for some good stories, anything to watch the lovely lady as she spoke, but she didn't seem too talkative. That disappointed him. As a widower, he didn't spend much time in the company of women, and he'd hoped for a lively conversation with Tenner's exquisite new bride.

"I see," he said, trying not to sound too disheartened. "Well, you have arrived safely and that is all that matters. Tell me, what do you think of your future husband? You should count yourself fortunate, my lady. Tenner de Velt could have any woman he wanted, but you are the one who has managed to capture the prize."

Annalyla was a little taken aback by the somewhat bold statement. She turned to look at Tenner, who was sitting on her right, and she smiled timidly.

"I do consider myself very fortunate, my lord," she said, for Tenner's ears more than the earl's. "The House of de Velt has a great name in the north. My father is particularly fond of your father, whom he considers a good friend. Odd how we have never met until now, considering we did not live very far from one another."

Tenner was looking at her, wishing the earl would shut his stupid mouth and go away. This was his bride and he wanted to speak with her, alone if he could. But Ivor was acting like a brilliant treasure had just dropped into their midst and he wanted to soak up all of it. Perhaps Tenner was just the slightest bit jealous, in truth, but now that the lady was speaking to him, he took charge.

"Roseden Castle is several miles to the south of Pelinom Castle, where I was born," he said, interjecting himself into the conversation whether or not Ivor liked it. "You have no other siblings, do you?"

Annalyla shook her head, happy that she was talking to Tenner and not the annoying earl. "I am an only child," she said. "But you have several siblings. I know your sister, Melisandra. When I was young, I remember attending parties at Castle Questing, the House of de Wolfe, and your mother would bring your sisters. Melly and I are nearly the same age. She was a lovely friend when I was young, but I've not seen her in years."

Tenner smiled faintly. "I remember those parties at Questing," he said. "I was much too old and important to attend them."

Annalyla giggled. "I do not see why," she said. "I can remember seeing a few young men there. Who else are the women to dance with?"

Tenner's smile grew. "Each other," he said. "Not me."

"Never?"

She was eyeing him rather impishly and he broke down into soft laughter. "I have never been one for dancing and parties, but I suppose if my wife wishes it, I should learn."

Annalyla beamed, and charm and warmth filled the air. "I should not force you to do anything you do not wish to do," she said. "If you hate dancing, *I* hate dancing."

"You are a sweet liar, my lady."

"Here, here," Ivor was incensed at being left out of the conversation. "If the lady wishes to dance, I shall dance with her. Is that your wish, my lady?"

The smile vanished unnaturally fast from Annalyla's face as she turned to the earl. Tenner saw it. He was at the end of his patience with Ivor competing for her attention and he found himself turning away, looking for Arlo or Maude. As Annalyla struggled to convince the earl that she was far too weary to dance and, most especially, without any music, Tenner located Arlo standing near the hall entry.

It didn't take much from Tenner to silently convey his displeasure at Ivor's meddling. Arlo understood in an instant. A faint nod of the head in Ivor's direction, and a flick of the hand that gestured towards the entry to the hall, and Arlo was already formulating a plan. So was Lady Maude, who had just joined him from the kitchens to see how the reception was going.

Pretty, pale Maude with the dark red hair and a neck like a swan. She saw Tenner's unhappy gestures and she leaned in to her husband, whispering, as Arlo nodded to whatever she was saying. Soon enough, both of them were moving for the table. But before they reached it, the faint sounds of screaming filled the air.

Everyone froze.

More screaming, sounding as if someone was dying. But the inhabitants of Seven Crosses only paused a brief moment; hardly breaking a stride, they continued on with their business as if the screams meant nothing. But to Annalyla, it was a worrisome sound.

"What was that?" she asked fearfully. "Is something happening?"

Movements resumed as Tenner shook his head. "Nay," he muttered. "Nothing is happening."

As Tenner tried to be discreet about it, Ivor wasn't so tactful. "If you remain at Seven Crosses any length of time, you will hear those sounds from time to time," he said. "Do not be alarmed."

Annalyla turned to him with wide, perhaps fearful eyes. "What is it?"

Ivor saw that he had control of the conversation again. "I have a daughter who is not of her right mind," he said. "She is confined to her chambers in the keep, but she does not like to remain there. You will hear her screaming from time to time."

Annalyla thought that sounded rather terrible. "I see," she said, pity in her voice. "I am so sorry. Is there anything that can be done?"

Ivor couldn't see that the lady was only being polite. He thought there was a private offer somewhere in those words, as if she had an interest in him personally. He was an earl, after all, and she was not yet married to Tenner. As he opened his mouth with a reply that perhaps would have upset the bridegroom greatly, Arlo was suddenly at the table.

"Tenner," he said evenly. "I have need of you. In private, if you will."

Tenner turned to Arlo, wondering what the man was up to, when Maude appeared on the other side of him, where Annalyla was. She smiled kindly at the young woman.

"My lady," she said. "I am Lady de Correa. I am sure you are quite weary from your journey. May I take you to a room where you can rest? Please come with me."

Everyone was moving; Tenner was on his feet, helping Annalyla to stand, while Ivor sat there, greatly distressed that the lovely angel was leaving him. He stood up, too, but Arlo waved him off, assuring him that he was not needed.

Very quickly, Tenner and Annalyla were escorted from the hall, with Mother Angel leaping up from her table and rushing to catch up. There was no way she was going to allow Annalyla to go anywhere without her. It was all quite chaotic as the group of them quit the hall to the chorus of more screams coming from the keep. Knowing what it was, Annalyla tried to ignore it.

"I *would* like to rest," she admitted to Maude, who had her by one arm as Tenner held the other. She looked over her shoulder to Mother Angel, scurrying behind her. "Mother Angel, can you make sure that my bags are taken to my chamber? I should like to change my clothing."

Mother Angel didn't want to leave her young charge alone, but she begrudgingly did as she was told. She came to a halt, watching a strange woman and the de Velt knight escort Annalyla towards the box-shaped keep before turning in the direction of the gatehouse where the St. Lo escort was still gathered, including the carriage.

But Annalyla wasn't paying attention to Mother Angel. She was far more interested in the keep, in her surroundings and, most of all, in Tenner. He was walking beside her, strong and proud, as tall as a tree. The knight who had summoned him was also walking beside him and made no move to take him away, to speak with him in private as he had indicated. It all seemed rather odd to Annalyla, but she didn't comment on it. She was simply glad they were free of the overly-attentive earl.

"Mother Angel," Tenner said, breaking into her train of thought. "Has she always been with you?"

Annalyla nodded. "My entire life."

Annalyla had no way of knowing that Tenner was thinking of Baiadepaura Castle and the prospect of having yet another female in residence at that awful place. Now that he'd seen Annalyla, he was more than willing to take her with him. Given the display he'd just seen with the earl, he had no intention of leaving her behind. But to take the nurse? He wasn't happy in the least, but he didn't want to upset Annalyla if she was particularly attached to the woman. He proceeded carefully.

"Is she part of your escort?" he asked. "Or is she to take residence in our household?"

Annalyla was quiet for a moment. "May I confide in you, my lord?"

"Please do."

She sighed. "Bringing Mother Angel into our household would be like bringing my mother," she said. "Most brides do not bring their mothers with them into a marriage, do they? She insisted on coming with me and now I am not sure how to be rid of her."

Before Tenner could answer, Maude replied. "That is a simple thing," she said, her brown eyes twinkling as she looked at Tenner. "Your new husband can send her away and there is naught she can do about it. If you ask Tenner, mayhap he will do this for you."

Annalyla smiled hesitantly, turning to Tenner, but he spoke before she could plead with him. "If you wish for me to send her away, I will do it," he said. "I agree with you. A marriage does not need a bride, a groom, *and* a mother. It would make the marriage far too crowded."

Annalyla felt a great deal of relief. Already, she was coming to like her betrothed. Not only was he handsome, but he seemed kind and reasonable. And she liked the way he looked at her, with a smile on his lips, as if there were already some consideration for her. There was warmth in his gaze like nothing she could have possibly imagined, not from a man who had been forced into this marriage just as she had been.

"I have never been away from Mother Angel," she said. "I have seen twenty-two years and, still, she will not leave me. If you could send her away, I think it would be much better for our marriage. I fear that she would only interfere, as she has always had complete charge of me. It will be difficult to see that duty go to another."

Tenner nodded as the wind caught his hair, blowing it away from the right side of his face. "Then say no more," he said. "Consider it done."

Annalyla caught sight of his right eye as the hair was whipped around by the wind. She saw the streak of bright green through it but, more than that, she had a good look at his entire face. The man was too beautiful for words.

"You have eyes like your sister," she said as they reached the entry to the keep. When the four of them paused, she lifted her hand to her right eye. "Melly has green in her eye like you do. I always thought it was so beautiful. I often wished I had such a thing."

Her comment caught Tenner off-guard and he snapped his head forward, purely out of habit, so the hair would fall forward and cover the right side of his face. It was an unsolicited and unexpected comment, spoken in a tone of genuine sincerity, and he had no idea what to say. He found that he was both embarrassed and flattered, but he was also wary. No one had ever said that to him before and, for a moment, he was actually speechless.

"I…" he began, caught himself, and then started again. "Maude will take you to rest. I must go and wait for the priest, and we shall be married as soon as he arrives."

The focus shifted away from his eye color as a ripple of surprise crossed Annalyla's features. "We are to be married today?"

Tenner nodded. "I will be taking a new post, a garrison for Lord Tiverton, and we must leave immediately. But we cannot leave without a wedding, so it shall take place today."

Annalyla was surprised at the rapidity of events, but she didn't say so. She simply nodded, already the obedient bride. Tenner flashed a stiff smile at her and turned on his heel, with Arlo beside him. Together, the men headed off towards the gatehouse, leaving Annalyla and Maude watching them go.

Maude was watching her husband for a moment, but turned to Annalyla to see that she was riveted to Tenner as the man headed off. Smiling, she reached out to take Annalyla by the elbow.

"He *is* rather handsome, my lady," she said softly. "Having never seen him before, I suppose you were not expecting such a thing."

Annalyla tore her eyes away from Tenner, flushing when she realized she'd been caught staring at him.

"I did not know what to expect," she admitted. "He seems very nice."

Maude grinned, pulling her into the entry. "He is," she said. "He will make a fine husband."

Annalyla sighed heavily. "I hope I make an equally fine wife."

Maude began to pull her up the stairs of the darkened keep. "I have a feeling you will do just fine."

Annalyla looked at her. "Do you really think so?"

Maude nodded. "You have a pleasing manner about you," she said. "Come along, now. You will rest before your wedding and while you do, I shall go to the kitchens and bring back some of the food you were denied when the earl tried to steal your attention away."

Annalyla *was* rather hungry. "The earl… is he always like that?"

Maude's smile faded. "Unfortunately," she said, but she refrained from saying anymore. "Come, now, no more talk of him. Let's find you some warm water and a bed."

Warm water and a bed. Both sounded lovely. But Annalyla's thoughts were still lingering on the enormous knight with the long, dark hair.

The man she was soon to marry.

CHAPTER FIVE

THE SCREAMING WOKE her up out of a dead sleep.

Howling was more like it. It took Annalyla a moment to orient herself, in a strange chamber and a strange bed, but she quickly realized where she was and why. She was at Seven Crosses Castle preparing to marry Tenner de Velt.

But something was wrong.

The first thing she realized was the rain pounding outside her window. It was spilling in, splashing on the floor. There were oil cloths on the windows, but they weren't doing a very good job at keeping out the driving rain. It had been clear weather when they'd arrived but, now, there was a tempest outside and foul weather was lashing the land as the skies went dark.

Leaping out of bed, Annalyla raced to the windows, securing the oil cloths as the wind whipped them around. Rain was splattering on the floor, on her, as she grabbed at them and secured them to the iron rods that ran perpendicular to the bottom of the window. She tied off first one, and then the other, shaking the water from her hands when she was finished.

It was quite a storm raging and she yawned, trying to wake up from her rest. She honestly had no idea how long she'd been asleep but assumed someone would have awoken her in time for her wedding. Tenner had said it would be as soon as the priest arrived, so perhaps the man had been delayed by the weather. In any case, she moved to the hearth, stoking it and bringing forth more of a bright blaze. There was a bank of fat tapers on the hearth and she lit them to bring some light into the chamber.

A gentle glow filled the room. Truthfully, it wasn't much of a chamber, and rather small, with only a bed in the middle of it. Her bags had been lined up neatly along the wall near the door, placed there by servants directed by Mother Angel. The old woman had promptly been removed from the room by Maude, who had taken a rather firm stance with Mother Angel when she wanted to stay.

Annalyla didn't know where Mother Angel was and, truthfully, she didn't care. She tried not to feel guilty over it. It was one of the rare occasions in her life that she was actually alone and the freedom was glorious. She found herself hoping Tenner really would send Mother Angel away, just as he'd promised, because Annalyla didn't need her any longer. She was a woman grown, about to embark on her new married life, and the last thing she wanted was a frustrated old shrew tagging along.

There was a small iron pot of water on an arm over the fire, heating up as the blaze licked at it. It was water Maude had put there; Annalyla had seen her do it. It was to wash with, so Annalyla rushed to her bags, those precious and expensive things her father had purchased with the last of their money, and began pulling them open, looking for the dress her father had made for her on the event of her wedding.

It was pale blue silk, with embroidery by Mother Angel on the long, belled sleeves, and a silver girdle for her waist. She came across it, carefully rolled up in canvas where Mother Angel had put it, and she unrolled it and shook it out, smiling as she laid it upon the bed. The wedding had been something she'd been dreading but with the event of handsome Tenner, she found that she was actually looking forward to it.

But thoughts of bringing deceit into her marriage grabbed at her, an unwelcome reminder. She found herself trying to rationalize it, imagining that, perhaps, they would be so happy that the acquisition of a destitute bride wouldn't matter to Tenner. Perhaps, she could make him so deliriously content that he wouldn't even care. But even as she tried to convince herself of such a thing, she knew that she was only fooling herself. Sooner or later, the lies would catch up to her, and to him. Like an ax hanging over their heads, eventually, it would fall.

It was a painful thought.

The thunder rolled and lightning lit up the sky, illuminating the room. As the water steamed, Annalyla tried to push aside thoughts of her deception yet again and pulled forth a precious piece of white soap wrapped in oil cloth. She was already stripped down to her shift, so she quickly washed her arms and neck, and under her arms and on her chest, freshening up so that she would smell pleasant for their marriage. Once she was washed and dried, she carefully wrapped the soap up and put it back in one of her bags, and went to the bed to pull the lovely wedding garment over her head.

It fit beautifully, emphasizing her rather curvy figure, and she was able to securely tie the laces of the girdle that were under her left arm. She never had maids, so dressing alone was habit with her. It was the one thing Mother Angel had never helped her with. With the dress on, she unbraided her hair and combed it thoroughly before braiding it again, winding matching ribbons into it as she listened to the rain outside. Thunder was breaking across the sky, booming, and shaking the very walls of the keep.

And then, she heard it again.

Screaming.

It's what had awakened her, that distant cry. Only this time, it seemed to be right outside her door. Startled, and the least bit afraid, Annalyla finished tying off the last ribbon in her hair and timidly made her way to the door. Putting her ear against the panel, she didn't hear anything, so she threw the bolt with the intention of seeing what was outside in the corridor. It was a foolish action, but natural curiosity drove her to it. The moment she opened the door, however, a body threw itself against the panel and the door very nearly slammed back.

Terrified, Annalyla threw all of her weight into the door, struggling to push it closed even as the person on the other side screamed and groaned. An arm was thrust into the gap between the door and the jamb as Annalyla wrestled to close it, and she could see that it was a pale arm, nearly translucent, with a hand that formed a claw. It was clawing everywhere, clawing for something to come into contact with, and clearly trying to hurt or mark whatever it could.

Nails like daggers.

That realization that sharp nails were slashing at her filled Annalyla with panic and, in a burst of energy, she slammed the door against the arm, listening to the person scream, with pain this time. It was obviously a woman, and as the woman pulled her arm out of the gap, Annalyla shoved the door shut and threw the iron bolt.

Outside the door, the screaming woman pounded and bellowed as Annalyla backed away from the door. As the thunder rolled and the wind howled, she was fearful that the madwoman at the door might actually be able to break the panel down. Scared for her very life, she looked around the room for a weapon, seeing the ash shovel near the hearth and rushing to collect it. It was made from heavy iron and she wielded it like a club, waiting for the madwoman to come crashing through. She was fully prepared to defend herself as the door rattled and shuddered.

But then, the movement abruptly stopped, and she could hear someone outside the door, firm voices against the madwoman's groans. The shovel was still in her hands as she stood there, trembling in fear, hearing the voices fade away. When all was silent, someone knocked heavily on her door.

"Lady Annalyla?"

It was Tenner. Still shaken, Annalyla answered the door with the shovel still in her hand. Wide eyes met with his somewhat grim expression.

"Is… is she gone?" she asked.

Tenner sighed in understanding, nodding. "She is," he said. "It looks as if you are prepared to do battle."

He was indicating the shovel in her hand and she looked at it as if suddenly remembering it. With a sigh of her own, this time of relief, she went to set it back down next to the hearth as Tenner took a few steps into the chamber.

"She tried to break in," Annalyla said. "Was that the earl's daughter?"

"Aye," Tenner said. "She managed to break free of her chamber when her minder was out of the room for a moment."

Annalyla looked at him. "Would she have tried to hurt me? She very nearly pushed the door in."

He scratched his head, displeasure evident in his manner. "It is doubtful," he said. "She has moments of violence but, mostly, she simply wants to break free of the keep. I've seen her bolt from the keep and then run circles out in the bailey until her minders are able to corral her."

Annalyla grew serious. "Has she always been like that?"

Tenner shook his head. "Nay," he said. "It's a rather sad story, in truth. Lady Jane FitzJohn was pledged to a knight a few years ago and before their wedding, she was thrown from her horse and hit her head. The injury was bad enough that it damaged her ability to speak and changed her manner somewhat. She has become what you see – a skittish creature. She and her knight were very fond of each other, but with her accident, Ivor refused the marriage between them. Eventually, he was banished from Seven Crosses. Maude thinks that it was his exile that finally drove Jane mad. We think she is trying to run from the keep to find him. Always trying to escape to him but never able to."

It was a tragic tale, indeed. "God's Bones," Annalyla muttered. "What a sorrowful thing to happen. Does she ever ask for him?"

"Listen to her when she screams. She is screaming his name – Beaufort."

It was a horrific thought and Annalyla gasped in sympathy. "How awful," she said. "Mayhap, she was trying to come in here to look for him, then."

"Possibly," Tenner said. He sighed faintly. "You see, Sir Beau de Fira was my friend. He was a fine man. It broke his heart when the physics gave him no hope for Jane's recovery even though he was fully willing to marry her. But Ivor was convinced that Beau's presence at Seven Crosses was agitating Jane, so he eventually banished the man. It is unfortunate for everyone; Jane was never like this before he left, only afterwards. The more she screams, the more Ivor locks her away."

Annalyla could see the shadow of pity in his features. "You believe the earl was wrong, then?"

Tenner nodded. "Aye," he said. "In fact, I have thought to recall Beau to Seven Crosses, for Jane's sake, but the earl will not hear of it. You must understand that I knew the pair well. Jane was vivacious and kind, and Beau was strong and dignified. What happened to them… it is a tragedy beyond measure. It may seem strange, but I have never quite gotten over what happened to them. To see a man and woman so perfect for each other, so adoring… even if the earl does not want Beau and Jane to be reunited, I do."

It was a distressing tale, to be sure, but a surprising bit of sentiment from a seasoned knight. Annalyla lingered on it, her thoughts on the proud young couple until tragedy struck. But as she pondered the worst, Tenner was watching her. She was out of the green wool traveling gown and dressed in a pale blue silk that was stunning, and he found himself looking at the way it draped over her body, which was round in all the right places. When she turned in his direction, he realized he was staring straight at her full breasts and quickly looked up at her face, hoping she didn't notice.

"I am sorry for your friend and for Lady Jane," she said. "But I am sure you did not come here to discuss such things. I hope I did not sleep too late. I was wearier than I thought. You could have sent someone to wake me."

Tenner's lips flickered with a smile. "Why?" he said. "The priest was delayed because of the storm. He has only just arrived, so there was no reason to wake you until then."

"I even slept through this terrible weather."

His smile broadened. "The weather here can turn in an instant," he said. "It is sunny one moment and howling the next."

"Do you like it better here than in Northumberland?"

He shrugged. "Better? Nay," he said. "It is different."

"Does it snow?"

"Sometimes in piles. In fact, if it becomes any colder, this rain might turn to ice. The weather here, if nothing else, is unpredictable."

It was small talk, and meaningless, and Annalyla was coming to think this was a perfect opportunity to speak openly, just the two of them. So far, they'd spent all of their time around other people and indulging in fairly superficial chatter, with no time alone. Though the mere fact he was here and they were unchaperoned, was considered improper.

But… she didn't very much care.

She relished the opportunity.

"If I may speak candidly, Sir Tenner," she said quietly. "I suspect this marriage was as much a surprise to you as it was to me, but I wanted you to know that I will do my best to ensure it is pleasant for the both of us."

His gaze drifted over her face. "On your father's order, of course."

My father wishes for me to maintain the illusion of St. Lo wealth any way I can, she thought. There was that horrible weight of guilt again, settling on her. And the more she looked at him, the more uneasy and tense she became.

She was about to do something terrible to an innocent man.

Annalyla had always had an unfailing sense of honesty. She'd learned it in her years of fostering at Netherghyll Castle, seat of the House of de Royans, and a mighty family with a strong sense of duty and moral strength. Those were the years she'd spent away from Mother Angel, seven glorious years, until she'd returned home and into the clutches of her father and Mother Angel once again. She'd truly loved her life at Netherghyll and it was only after she'd returned home that she discovered her return had been at her father's demand. He wanted his daughter home, his only child, and Annalyla found herself back at Roseden, back with people who said they loved her but only wanted to control her.

That was Mother Angel's grip on her.

That was why she was so grateful that Tenner agreed to send the woman away. Annalyla had to breathe; she had to be able to live her own life. But because of her years at Netherghyll, and spending those years with people who truly cared about her and who were truly righteous and generous in their teachings, she was coming to seriously wonder if she could go through with all of this.

She realized that she couldn't.

She needed to take a stand.

Tenner de Velt was entering into a marriage under false pretenses. That was established. It was also established that it was something that had disturbed Annalyla from the start. She'd stewed about it for the past year, and never more than in the journey south. But Mother Angel had been there, insisting it was what she must do to ensure the survival of her family. But now that Mother Angel wasn't around to twist her arm and shoot her terrible glares, she felt much braver. The moral compass in her demanded she confess the situation to Tenner. It would cost her the marriage, but it was either that or spend her days fearful of the moment when he would discover that he'd married a penniless heiress.

It was the only decent thing to do, and she knew it.

God help her… she knew it.

"Aye," she said after a moment. "He did tell me to say that. But before we go through with this marriage, there is something you must know. Will you hear me, my lord?"

Tenner thought she seemed rather edgy as she spoke and several unhappy reasons jumped to mind, but one in particular; they'd both been pulled into this marriage by their fathers, and he thought that, perhaps, Annalyla was more averse to it than he was. Worse still, perhaps she had a lover, something that was making her emotional and resistant to the marriage to Tenner. She was such a beautiful woman and, from all accounts, sweet and gentle.

Of course she had a lover. What man wouldn't give his all to be with her? His heart sank as he thought that was what he was about to hear.

"Of course," he said calmly. "I will always hear you. And it would please me if you would call me Tenner. Addressing me formally seems odd under these circumstances."

Annalyla flashed him a weak smile. Then, she turned for her bags, making her way over to the heavy green cloak that was hanging on a peg on the wall. She fingered it.

"I should not tell you this," she said. "In doing so, I am going against my father's wishes and all I have been schooled on, but I find… Tenner, you seem like a kind and understanding man. And to say that I am honored by this betrothal is truly an understatement. I could not imagine anything more wonderful. You are a fine knight with a great destiny as a son of de Velt. And because of that, I cannot let you enter into a marriage that is not what it seems. For your sake, you must know the truth."

He was both flattered and curious. "What truth, my lady? Please speak."

She breathed in deeply, closing her eyes for a moment as she did so. The heavy cloak came off the peg and she turned towards him. "If you wish to refuse this betrothal, I am about to give you the grounds for it. You should not be forced into something that is a lie."

"Then tell me what it is that is a lie."

Annalyla was having difficulty looking at him. "My father is a kind man," she said. "He is a well-liked man and the name of St. Lo is well respected. That is why my father approached your father for this marriage. He hoped your father would be open to it because of our family's reputation. We own a great deal of land between Wooler and Powburn, but I am sorry to say, through wars and my father's mismanagement, that is all we have to our name. You are betrothed to an heiress, my lord, but it is only in name. Other than the lands, we have nothing more to offer. The coffers are empty. You see the last of our money in this wardrobe I wear, in this cloak in my arms, because my father wanted to create the illusion that there is still money for you to inherit. I had every intention of keeping this illusion, but I find that I cannot. It is cruel and dishonest. Therefore, if… if you will simply write a missive to my father that you are refusing the betrothal for reasons of your own, I will return home and take it to him. He need not know that I told you the truth. It will save my dignity and yours."

She was looking at the floor by the time she finished. Tenner stood by the bed, absorbing the words that had been delivered in a rather shaky voice. She was upset, he could tell, but the truth was that her words had little meaning to him. None at all, in fact. He found himself relieved and rather thrilled that she hadn't told him about a lover she'd left behind.

All she seemed concerned with was the fact that he was inheriting some useless land when he married her. But he saw it quite differently. He saw it as inheriting *her*. Lies or not, intrigue or not, she had his attention and even though he'd barely spent any time with her, his instincts told him that he didn't want to let her get away. Beauty aside, only a truly honest and true woman would have confessed to him what she'd just confessed. She was giving up the chance to save herself, and her family, because she felt truth was more important than her own well-being.

To him, that was worth more than any inheritance.

"Do you really think that I would send you back?" he asked, somewhat incredulous.

Her head came up. "You…" she stammered. "Why wouldn't you? I have just told you that there is no money. My father lied."

Tenner lifted his big shoulders. "Men lie all the time," he said. "I am sure my father lied, too, when he told your father that I was the most eligible bachelor in England. I'm not, you know. So do not think your father was the only one who lied his way into this betrothal. I am sure my father did, too, thinking he was obtaining the great St. Lo heiress for me. So, in truth, the joke is on my father."

With that, he started to laugh, a truly melodic laugh that bubbled up from his toes, low and sultry. Annalyla stared at him in astonishment, at the big, white teeth and the smile that dramatically changed his face. It only made him more handsome.

"Then… then you are not angry?" she asked in surprise.

He was still chuckling. "Of course not," he said. Then, he sobered quickly. "Unless you wish to return home. Do you wish to return home? If you do, I'll not keep you here. I'll tell your father I refused the betrothal if you wish."

Annalyla was having difficulty believing none of this mattered to him. "None of this is of issue to you? The fact that I have only the clothes on my back and the semblance of the St. Lo good name?"

He'd stopped laughing, only a smile lingering on his lips. "It matters not to me," he said. "Does it matter to you?"

She struggled for an answer. "I do not know what to say to that," she said truthfully. "I have been wrestling with this deception for an entire year, knowing what was expected of me. I was resigned to going through with it until I met you and then… then I simply couldn't deceive you so. If Mother Angel knew I'd told you the truth, she would box my ears."

His smile vanished. "She'll not touch you," he said. "I shall send her back to your father with a missive thanking him for entrusting his lovely daughter to me. And that is the only missive I shall send. You are going to marry me and we'll worry no more of the St. Lo inheritance, or lack thereof. I will inherit Pelinom Castle when the time comes. I do not need any more wealth. But I do need a wife, and you will do nicely."

Annalyla was still astonished but, slowly, she was coming to realize he was serious. He wasn't throwing fits, or worse, throwing her out on her ear. He was quite serious about what he was saying and the more she thought on it, the more overwhelmed she became. With a heavy sigh, she made her way over to the bed and sank onto it because there were no chairs in the room. She found that she had to sit and think about what had just happened.

Was the man truly so forgiving?

"If you are quite sure," she said. "And you do not feel coerced?"

"Nay."

"Trapped?"

"Not in the least."

"Then if you are quite sure, I will again say what I said when we first met – I am deeply honored, Sir Tenner. That was not a lie."

The smile returned to his lips as he gazed at her a moment before lowering himself to the bed beside her. He just looked at her, the hair hanging over the right side of his face like it always did, and Annalyla stared at him in return.

"Honesty is the greatest quality I could ask for next to loyalty," he said. "You have proven that you are honest. I suspect you will easily prove that you are loyal as well."

"I shall, I swear it."

"Good," he said. "We have quite a destiny, you and I. You must be brave to face it."

She nodded, watching the colors in his dark hair reflect the candlelight. "I believe I am brave," she said. "I have always tried to be. I told you about my father, didn't I?"

He conceded the point. "That is true," he said. "But after we are married this night, we embark on a new adventure that is going to require all of your courage and your obedience. I mentioned earlier that I was to assume a new post; to be truthful, when Tiverton told me of my new assignment, I did not want to take my new wife with me. I did not want to take *any* woman with me, for my new outpost is no place for a woman. But in the short time we have known one another, you have shown me courage. I think you will do well."

She cocked her head. "Why would you not want to take your wife to a new outpost? Is it dangerous?"

Tenner thought of the piracy, the wildness of the area surrounding Baiadepaura. "All of Cornwall is dangerous," he said. "It is a wild place."

"That is what Graham told me."

"Who is Graham?"

"My father's knight," she said. "He is the one who escorted me here. His grandfather was from Cornwall. In fact, Graham was telling me the stories of piskies and haunted castles on the journey here."

Tenner lifted a dark eyebrow. "There are many such tales," he said. "It seems as if every town and every corner in Cornwall and western Devon has some manner of legend associated with it. Where we are going most definitely has a legend."

"Where are we going?"

"A place called Baiadepaura Castle."

Annalyla's eyes widened. "That is one of the castles that Graham told me about!" she gasped. "He said the lord of Baiadepaura was burned to death for bringing a plague. He said the castle is cursed!"

Tenner's lips flickered with a smile at the look of fright on her face. "I thought you were brave."

She tried very hard to quell her reaction, not wanting to look like a superstitious fool in front of him. "I am," she insisted. "But you just told me that you did not wish to bring a wife to Baiadepaura. If you do not believe in the curse, why would you say that?"

He fought off a grin. "Because it sits on a coast plagued with pirates," he said flatly. "That is the only reason. Pirates make it dangerous, especially since the place has remained vacant for so long. It will be up to me to restore Baiadepaura Castle and make it a powerful outpost to protect Tiverton's properties."

The way he said it suggested that he was rather confident in his abilities. What was it Graham had said about the House of de Velt? *A de Velt can tame anything.* Simply looking at Tenner, Annalyla was willing to believe that.

She was willing to believe in *him*.

"Then… then you do not believe Baiadepaura is cursed?" she asked.

Tenner shrugged, a noncommittal gesture. "Who is to say that we are not all cursed to come degree?" he said. "I prefer to believe in men and their evils, not ghosts and their evils. If I cannot see it, then it therefore does not exist. But if I can see it, I can fight it. And I will win."

He sounded so confident, reminding Annalyla very much of the knights she once knew at Netherghyll Castle. Confident and certain they could conquer the world. Tenner had much that same energy. And even though Graham had told her that Baiadepaura was a terrible place, Tenner's refusal to give in to any suggestions of curses made her feel comforted. If he wasn't worried, then she wasn't going to be, either.

"I believe you," she said. "And we leave tomorrow?"

He nodded, rising from the bed. "Tomorrow before sunrise," he said. "In fact, the priest is awaiting us in the great hall to perform the marriage ceremony and Maude has arranged a feast. She and Arlo are going with us to Baiadepaura, so you will have a companion."

Annalyla liked that idea a great deal. "I am so glad," she said. "It will be lovely coming to know Maude. And you."

He gave her a little smirk, reaching out to tap the end of her nose. It was a sweet little gesture, almost one of affection. Annalyla would have been very happy to believe it was an affectionate gesture had she known the man any longer than just a few hours. Even so, there was no denying the warmth between them, especially after she confessed her father's terrible intentions. His acceptance and forgiveness of the deception in the marriage had endeared her to him more than anything she could have dreamed of.

She didn't care that they were going to Baiadepaura Castle. She would have followed him anywhere.

"We shall have the rest of our lives to know one another," he said. "Until a few hours ago, it was something I wasn't looking forward to. But now, I am. If you are prepared to begin that journey, my lady, then

I am prepared to escort you."

Annalyla nodded eagerly and retrieved her cloak from where she'd put it. When she went to sling it over her shoulders, Tenner took it from her and placed it on her himself. He even fastened the ties beneath her chin. Giving her a smile, perhaps one that suggested he'd suddenly realized he was about to become a married man. He took her by the elbow and led her towards the chamber door. The minute he opened it, however, they both heard a plaintive howl over the rain.

Annalyla's good humor faded as she heard the screaming again. Lady Jane was back to her screeching ways. But now that she understood the story behind it, she felt a great deal of pity for the woman. She could only imagine how she would feel were she denied her marriage to Tenner. It wasn't as if she loved the man but, already, her heart was full at the prospect of a new life with him. She felt so very sorry that Lady Jane had missed out on that with her lover. As the screams rose in tandem with the bursts of thunder, she could hear the lover's name piercing the noise of the storm.

"*Beauuuuuuuuuuuuufort!*"

It was as clear as a bell now.

A tragic sound, indeed.

CHAPTER SIX

MOTHER ANGEL WOULDN'T stop her weeping.

In truth, Annalyla was in shock. She'd never seen the woman show much emotion other than varied levels of disdain and frustration, so to see her weeping after the soaking-wet priest completed the wedding mass was something of a surprise.

It told Annalyla that the woman was human, after all.

She'd had her doubts. In all of the years she'd spent with Mother Angel hovering over her, there had rarely been any warmth or emotion, so she found that she was actually angry that the woman should become so emotional over her marriage to Tenner. To her, it was false emotion, making a show of it, and Annalyla didn't like that. She genuinely had no need for the woman any longer.

She wanted her gone.

Now that she was married, she could indeed send her away, and Tenner would do so without hesitation. But she wanted Graham to remain. She'd always had a great deal of respect for the man and she asked Tenner if he would give the man the option to remain as part of the Tiverton force. After Tenner discussed it with Arlo and Ivor, he agreed to accept Graham's fealty as part of Annalyla's dowry. Considering he was really the only thing of value she had, he was happy to take that from Cain St. Lo.

He considered it fair payment for the inheritance the old man had tried to cheat him out of.

Leaving his new wife enjoying the feast that Maude had arranged on the event of their marriage, Tenner went to the table in the corner that contained Mother Angel, Graham, and the small St. Lo escort. They were informed that they were to leave on the morrow after the horses were properly fed and rested, but that they were not to linger at Seven Crosses.

As Mother Angel stopped her wailing and glared at her charge's new husband, Tenner pulled Graham aside and informed him of his change in duties to serve the new Lady de Velt and her husband. Graham had a split second of indecision followed by complete agreement. Even though he'd not wanted to leave Cain St. Lo, or the destitute house he'd always served, Tenner's proposal had been an unexpected one. He liked the idea of a little adventure in his later life. No wife, his sons seeking their own fortune, and he was apt to change his future as well. All it had taken was a solid offer.

And he wasn't sorry.

Meanwhile, Mother Angel kept trying to leave her table to approach Annalyla, but Arlo kept her at her table with the other St. Lo attendants. As the night went on, the old woman drank heavily, so much so that Maude finally leaned in to Annalyla as they sat next to one another, surrounded by men in conversation.

"Your nurse does not look too happy, Lady de Velt," Maude commented. "At any moment, she shall be shooting daggers from her eyes at you."

Annalyla wouldn't look at Mother Angel. There was a part of her that didn't want to tell the woman that Tenner knew everything of the intended marital deceit, because there was that inherent fear; she had feared the woman as a child. Mother Angel had been in complete control and that child in Annalyla didn't want to disappoint her. But there was great freedom in the realization that she didn't have to fear her any longer, that she was now a married woman, and Mother Angel held no power over her. Out of pure courtesy and nothing more, she thought she should speak to the woman before she was sent back to Roseden and tell her everything.

There was some satisfaction in that, knowing there could be no retribution.

"She has been my nurse since I was an infant," she said after a moment. "She has always acted as if she were my mother, and I suppose she believes she is."

Maude lingered on her for a moment. "But you are not close to her."

Annalyla shook her head. "Not really," she said, looking to Maude. "Please do not think me cruel. You must understand that Mother Angel has been a great manipulator for my entire life. The woman does not have a warm bone in her body. She has ice in her veins and a stone where her heart should be. Think not that she is crying because there is any emotion involved; she is weeping because she is losing the ability to control me. For that, and no other reason."

Maude forced a smile, her gaze moving to the weeping woman across the hall. "I was raised by my grandmother," she said. "We were always quite close. I am sorry you've not had that experience."

"As am I."

"What happened to your mother?"

"She withdrew from life soon after I was born. She lives, still, but she chooses not to have anything to do with me or with my father. That is why Mother Angel has filled the role."

Maude looked at her, feeling rather sorry for the woman that she'd spent the better part of the evening coming to know. Annalyla was bright, and had a streak of humor in her, and seemed eager to please. Maude liked her already and she could tell that Tenner was quite interested in his new bride, which was a change from the man who had been ambivalent since receiving word of the betrothal last year.

He was ambivalent no longer.

Maude was quite fond of Tenner even though the man had usurped her husband's position those years ago when Ivor had brought him from Surrey. But the humble and skilled knight had won them all over. Maude was glad that Annalyla was kind and earnest in her desire to please; it made Maude's life easier, since Annalyla technically would outrank her. She was happy to be subservient to a woman she liked as opposed to a woman she would want to strangle.

"Well," she finally said. "It seems as if everyone must look forward to a new life ahead, including your nurse and including you. Did Tenner tell you that Arlo and I are coming to Baiadepaura with you?"

Annalyla nodded, smiling at the woman that she was coming to like. "I am very happy to hear that," she said. "I helped my father run his home of Roseden Castle, but it is a small place. Certainly not the size of Seven Crosses. It is clear you manage Seven Crosses quite competently."

Maude grinned. "You are kind," she said. "Truly, there is no one else to do it. When Arlo and I were married, Lady Jane was chatelaine in the wake of her mother's death, but since her troubles began, the duty fell to me. I do not mind, except when Ivor interferes. In truth, it will be a relief to get away from Seven Crosses."

Annalyla sensed something more to her statement, something she'd alluded to earlier. "You mean get away from the earl?" she said, keeping her voice low. "He seemed quite… solicitous earlier, but he has hardly spoken to me since the wedding."

Maude glanced down the table to where Ivor sat between Tenner and Arlo, drinking his way into oblivion.

"That is because Arlo probably told him that his attention on a new bride would not be well met," she said quietly. She was hesitant to continue. "I am certain that Tenner will tell you, but allow me to say that the earl can be improper at times. Since his wife died, he lives and breathes for the company of a woman. I simply stay away from him, but when you came, he saw his chance to speak to you even before Tenner had. It is not his fault; he is simply lonely. But you would do well not to be alone with him. He does not know when enough is enough."

That explained a little about the earl's boorish behavior. "I thank you for telling me," she said softly. "Since we are leaving tomorrow for Baiadepaura, it will not be an issue, but I thank you for confiding in me just the same. Truly, I feel some pity for the man – a mad daughter, and with him living such a lonely existence… it must be so miserable at times."

Maude nodded. "I agree," she said. "But I am happy to be going to Baiadepaura with you. You and I shall be great friends, I think."

Annalyla nodded. "I hope so," she said. "I think we are already. It will be great fun."

"I think so."

"My lady?"

It was Tenner, on the other side of Annalyla, cutting into the conversation. Both women turned to see him smiling at them, with his familiar appearance of half of his hair hanging over the right side of his face. When his one eye met with Annalyla's attention, his smile broadened.

"We have a very early start on the morrow, so we would do well to retire," he said to her. "The escort is being prepared tonight so they will be ready to leave before sunrise."

Annalyla nodded. "Who else is coming with us other than Sir Arlo and Lady Maude?"

Tenner pointed to the St. Lo escort across the room. "I am taking Graham," he said. "I spoke to the man a little. He knows the area we are going to, having spent time there as a child, so his knowledge will prove valuable. I am also taking five hundred men from Seven Crosses, so it will be a rather large escort."

Annalyla was pleased that Graham was coming with them. "I am surprised he agreed to come, considering it was he who told me such frightening stories."

Tenner grinned. "He has little choice now," he said. "He tried to scare you with those tales and now he must face the consequences of his actions. If my wife is climbing the walls in terror, then I will make him talk you down."

Annalyla started laughing. "Graham has three sons and a rather fatherly manner. He did not mean to scare me with those tales. Moreover, it did not work. I was not frightened."

"Not even a little?"

"Nay."

"That is good." Tenner stood up, pulling Annalyla to her feet. "Bid Maude a good eve and we shall see her on the morrow."

Annalyla did, departing the table after also bidding Ivor and Arlo a farewell. Drunk, Ivor wanted to know why she was leaving her own wedding feast so early, but Tenner was able to explain the situation enough so that the earl understood. Ivor was unhappy, but he understood. Dealing with a drunk earl was not a rarity around Seven Crosses. They'd all had to deal with it from time to time.

As Ivor sat at the table to drown himself in more sweet wine, Tenner took his new wife by the elbow and began escorting her from the hall. He'd hoped to avoid the usual catcalls and lewd comments that were standard on a wedding night, but there was no such luck. The men of Seven Crosses were well into their wine, and their gambling games, and when they saw the bride and groom leaving, they immediately tried to follow as Tenner held up a hand to stave off the tide of overeager men. Annalyla, unaware of what he was doing, came to a halt as he tried to get her out of the hall.

"I was hoping to bid Mother Angel a final farewell," she said, looking over to the St. Lo table. "She has been with me my entire life and although I have no great love for her, I feel that I should at least bid her farewell. May I?"

Tenner could see the surge of men coming towards them. But against his better judgement, he realized that he couldn't deny her. Her sweet voice and polite request immediately had him surrendering, the speed of which surprised even him. He wasn't the type to be swayed by a woman, in any case, but he found he couldn't refuse her.

With a growl, he nodded and turned in the direction of the St. Lo table.

Mother Angel saw them coming. She'd been watching her charge as the woman headed towards the hall entry, but when she suddenly shifted course in her direction, Mother Angel stood up. She came away from the table as Annalyla approached and left Tenner standing a few feet away so that she could speak to the woman alone. In the noise and heat of the hall, the two women faced one another.

"Are you well, child?" Mother Angel demanded quietly. "They would not let me go to you, not all day. Have your needs been met? Are you comfortable?"

Annalyla nodded. "I am fine," she said. "Tomorrow, I leave with my husband for his new post. I will not see you again."

Mother Angel sighed sharply. "He told me," she said, her voice low. "You must demand that I accompany you. It is crucial."

Annalyla shook her head. "It was I who told him to send you home," she said, watching the old woman's features tighten. "I am a married woman now, Mother Angel. I no longer need your guidance, though I appreciate what you have done for me."

It was a gracious lie, for the most part. She didn't appreciate the pressure and manipulation the old woman had heaped upon her. But to be pleasant, she lied. She watched Mother Angel's eyes widen.

"Are you mad?" the old woman hissed. "You know nothing. You need me, child. Don't be stupid!"

Annalyla could see that this was going to deteriorate quickly. Letting out a breath, she took a step back, moving away from the increasingly angry old woman.

"I do not need you and I do not want you," she said clearly. "Return to my father and tell him you have completed your duty. You have delivered me to my husband, who is now in charge of my welfare. And you can also tell my father that I told Tenner everything. He knows there is no more money. He is aware that Father tried to deceive him."

Mother Angel's mouth popped open in outrage. "*What* did you do?"

"I told you. My husband knows that my father lied about the money. He knows there is nothing but the good St. Lo name."

Mother Angel lashed out a hand, grabbing Annalyla by the wrist. But the moment she did so, Tenner was there. He reached out and grabbed the old woman's arm, squeezing so hard that bones cracked. As Mother Angel screamed and let go of Annalyla, Tenner pulled his wife back, out of the vicious old lady's grip.

"Your days of being cruel to her are over," he growled at Mother Angel. "Be grateful that I did not rip your arm from its socket. Return to Roseden and tell Lord Cain that his daughter is now in good hands, with people who will treat her with kindness and honesty. And if I ever see you again, run the other way. You will not like our encounter. I showed restraint just now. In the future, I shall have no such reserve."

With that, he took Annalyla by the arm and escorted her from the hall, leaving Mother Angel weeping over an injured arm, and the hall in general confusion. Some men were looking at the old woman curiously, while most of them were thinking they should follow the newlywed couple to the keep. Their enthusiasm for their wedding night was not dampened.

Tenner, however, had other ideas. He held out a hand to them, basically stopping them from following, but that didn't prevent them from shouting husbandly encouragement to him. He would have been amused by it had he not been so angry with his new wife's former nurse. The idea of anyone putting a hand on Annalyla in anger did not sit well with him. As he helped her put on her cloak before they headed out into the storm, he was surprised when she suddenly put her soft hands on his forearms.

"She did not hurt me," she said steadily. "Your defense of me was quite noble, but she did not hurt me, I promise."

He eyed her, feeling her warm hands on him like branding irons. He thought it rather intuitive that she could sense his protective anger. "But she has done that to you before. I could tell."

Annalyla didn't lie to him. "She was always quick with a switch or a slap if she was displeased. It is simply her way."

"And you were forced to tolerate it."

She didn't say anything; she simply looked up at him, a thin smile on her lips, and that was answer enough. It made Tenner's blood boil, what he knew of the nurse and his new wife's father, to think of that pair manipulating and abusing her. He didn't know all of it. In fact, he really didn't know any of it, but he would. In the days to come, he would. And he swore she would never know such exploitation again.

His brave, truthful lady would know peace.

It was still raining outside as they crossed the bailey to the box-shaped keep. Annalyla clutched Tenner as they moved through the mud, and he finally bent over and picked her up simply to keep her skirts dry. He was ankle-deep in the mud and didn't want her getting too wet or too dirty if he could help it, so he did the gallant thing and carried her straight into the keep.

Once inside the door, he set her to her feet.

"My thanks," Annalyla said, brushing bits of mud from the bottom of her cloak. "That was very kind of you."

He helped her brush off some of the dirt from the bottom. "It was nothing," he said. "You are as light as a feather. How can I show you my amazing strength if you do not weigh more?"

She laughed softly. "I apologize," she said. "Remind me of this moment in years to come when I am round and ungainly, and you are old and feeble. I shall expect you to carry me everywhere."

It was his turn to laugh as he turned her towards the stone steps that led to the floor above. "I can only imagine that you will always be young and beautiful in my eyes," he said. "Is that what a husband is supposed to say?"

"A smart one does."

He continued to snort all the way up to her small, borrowed chamber, which would become his, at least for what they were about to do. He intended to consummate the marriage immediately and then return to his duties of organizing the army that would march forth into Cornwall on the morrow. Even now, Arlo was heading out to start the process while Graham had been instructed to see to the St. Lo escort before going to help Arlo.

In truth, Tenner wasn't thinking of the escort being assembled, or anything else at the moment, other than the lovely creature he'd married earlier in the evening. It was true that he could wait to consummate the marriage, but he honestly didn't want to. Perhaps that was selfish of him, but the lady had intrigued him since he'd met her and he wanted to get his hands on what now belonged to him. He saw no reason to wait unless she seemed particularly upset about it. If that was the case, then he would wait until she was comfortable.

But it would surely test his patience.

As they entered the small chamber, it was dark and somewhat cold. Tenner went to stoke the fire as Annalyla removed the heavy green cloak and hung it on the peg. The storm outside was blowing chilled wind through the gaps in the oil cloths, and she rubbed at her arms, suddenly feeling self-conscious now that they were out of the hall and away from the crowd. It was just the two of them and she knew what needed to take place.

Annalyla wasn't totally naïve of relations between a husband and wife. She'd first caught wind of the ways of men and women at Netherghyll from giddy maids, and then from Mother Angel once she'd returned to Roseden. Mother Angel had instructed her to simply lie still, spread her legs, and let her husband do as he pleased. It had been a crude but somewhat honest explanation.

It was advice she intended to follow.

Oddly, she wasn't afraid. She was actually quite curious. Tenner had been kind and gracious from the start and she expected this to be no different. She was his wife now, and consummating the marriage was expected. He'd accused her of being brave and, in this case, she would make sure she didn't disappoint, even if the anticipation of the unknown was doing flip-flops in her belly.

Near the hearth, Tenner crouched down as he put peat upon the embers. Annalyla's gaze drifted over him; he was still in the pale tunic and leather breeches he had on when she first met him, and she could see his broad back as it strained against the tunic. Big arms, big muscles… everything about him was big, and oh-so-beautiful.

Her husband.

She could hardly believe it.

Thinking she should probably undress, she unfastened the ties of the pale blue dress and loosened it enough to pull it over her head. She had a lamb's wool sheath on underneath, and she kept it on as she headed to the bed, all the while watching Tenner as he built up the fire into a nice blaze. By the time he stood up and turned around, she was already climbing into bed.

"I can imagine it has been an exhausting day for you," he said, simply to make conversation. "I fear tomorrow will be a long day as well."

Annalyla pulled the coverlet up to her chest, clutching it against her body. "How long will it take for us to reach Baiadepaura?"

He moved to the bed, loosening his tunic in preparation for removing it. "At least three days," he said. "In this weather, we will move slowly. I do not want to bring a carriage, so you will ride a palfrey. Or you can ride with me. It is your choice."

Of course, she could ride her own horse, but riding with him seemed so much more… agreeable. She wanted to be close to him. Still, she didn't want to come across as helpless.

"I am sure you do not wish to have my burden upon your horse," she said. "I can ride a palfrey if you wish it. It may be better for you if I do, considering how bad the weather is."

He pulled the tunic over his head, revealing a muscular chest and arms, and a beautifully trim torso. In fact, Annalyla looked at him with some surprise because she hadn't much exposure to men being naked from the waist up, and certainly not a man who was standing so close to her. It brought home the reality of what they were about to do.

Now, the nerves came.

"I am comfortable either way, although you may be more comfortable on your own animal," he said. Looking up, he caught the expression on her face as she looked at his nude torso, and he fought off a grin. She looked a bit like a startled deer. "You *do* realize that we are speaking of everything but what we have come into this chamber to do. God help us, we are speaking of the weather and riding palfreys."

Annalyla tore her eyes away from his smooth skin, seeing that he was trying very hard not to smile. They were really being quite ridiculous, each one trying to avoid the subject at hand like it was nothing of consequence, and she started to laugh.

"Forgive me," she said, feeling silly and embarrassed, "but this is all quite new to me. I have been told what to expect, but… well, I suppose I am doing what I think I am supposed to do. I am supposed to get into bed, am I not?"

He snorted. "Aye," he said. "That is usual."

"You have done this before, then?"

He looked at her in shock before his grin returned. Now, he was feeling embarrassed. "You are making assumptions."

"Not really. I am hoping you know what to do, because I certainly do not. If we both do not know what to do, then this evening may end very quickly."

His laughter returned, for she was quite humorous in her observation. "That is quite true," he said. "But have no fear; I have asked around. I know what to do."

"Then you have not done this before?"

He sighed, a sign that he was reluctant to answer her. "Do you truly wish to speak of this now?"

Annalyla shook her head. "I just want to make sure you are not expecting me to take the lead."

"I am not expecting you to take the lead."

They looked at each other and started laughing all over again. It was a charming moment, one that loosened Annalyla tremendously because it seemed to her that he was possibly nervous in all of this, too. Sitting down on the bed, Tenner proceeded to remove his boots, followed very shortly by his breeches. Annalyla was watching him until that point, but when she saw him slide his breeches down, she began to panic a little. Then, she pulled the coverlet over her face to block the rather shocking view. She could hear him chuckle.

"Is it that bad, then?"

She was growing increasingly anxious. "Of course not," she said. "I was simply giving you some privacy."

The coverlet abruptly yanked back, off of her face, and there he stood, as naked as a newborn infant. Annalyla couldn't help but look at his flat belly and the dark growth of hair around his groin. She was nearly at eye level with it. His male member was already semi-engorged, which made it look rather massive to her.

The humor fled as she looked up at his face. He seemed to be looking at her rather seriously, too. But without a word, he climbed into bed and pulled the coverlet up around them both.

For a moment, they simply lay there, looking at each other. They were beyond the laughter, now, the jesting to lighten the mood. Now, the moment was upon them and there was nothing funny about it, only intense and unadulterated curiosity and attraction. When Annalyla smiled timidly, he smiled in return.

"May I proceed, Lady de Velt?" he whispered.

All Annalyla could do was nod. With his wife's permission, Tenner leaned forward, capturing her sweet lips in his own for a gentle kiss. It was only meant to be an introduction, a foretaste of what was to come. But the moment he touched her, it was as if something in him snapped and he slid forward to pull her into his arms. Body to body, they touched, and his kisses increased in intensity as he embraced her tightly, feeling her warmth in his arms with the greatest of pleasure.

But he needed more. It wasn't long before his grip on her loosened, and a hand moved down her arm, to her torso, and ended up on her belly. Her skin was like silk. As his lips continued to suckle hers, acquainting her with not only his kisses, but with his touch, the hand on her belly moved to the underswell of her breast.

Annalyla gasped softly as she felt his hand against her bosom, pulling back to look at him. There was some fear in her eyes. Tenner gazed back at her before dipping low to gently kiss her cheek, wordlessly easing that fear. As he nuzzled her soft skin, his hand moved up and fully enclosed her right breast against the palm. He squeezed gently, fondling her, and Annalyla's initial resistance was quickly stilled when she realized how much she liked it.

Tenner heard her groan and, quick as a flash, he pulled her shift over her head. Now, it was her naked skin against his, and his kisses resumed. The hand on her naked breast grew bolder. Soon enough, Tenner's mouth was on her soft white cleavage and his palm fondled her naked breast. A taut nipple rubbed against his hand, and when he could no longer stand it, his hot mouth descended upon it, suckling furiously.

It was a sensation beyond belief. Annalyla cried out softly as his hot, wet mouth pulled at her nipple. In the process, he had managed to wedge himself in between her legs, his big body overwhelming her. Everything he was doing was new and wonderful and wicked.

She wanted more.

So did Tenner. He was in haze of lust and attraction as he felt her respond to him, her small hands in his inky hair. Her flesh was sweet and he nursed hungrily at her breasts, first one and then the other. He'd never been so wildly aroused in his entire life. Had he done this before? Of course he had. But not like this.

Never like this.

Moving down her torso, he dragged his tongue across her soft flesh. He could smell the delicious musky scent of her woman's center and there was nothing stopping him from reaching that forbidden fruit. It belonged to him now, and he would have it. Grasping her buttocks with both hands, his mouth descended on the pink folds between her legs.

Annalyla shrieked softly as Tenner's tongue forged into virgin territory. Shocked, the words of protest died on her lips when she quickly realized how pleasurable it was. He was stroking her with his tongue and Annalyla was overcome with it. She squirmed beneath him, becoming acquainted with Tenner in a way she could have never imagined. It was all so new and naughty but, in the same breath, she had never known anything so wonderful existed.

As Tenner suckled her tender folds, Annalyla could feel something building in her loins, something that promised utter pleasure should she only submit. All she knew was that Tenner held the key to whatever it was she needed, and she was completely submissive to his desires.

She was a willing captive.

Then, that marvelous release began. She could feel it starting deep in her loins, something pulsating and warm. Tenner could feel the start of her climax and he lifted himself up, thrusting his manhood into her wet and warm passage. She was so primed for his body that there was very little pain when he breached her maidenhead. More than that, there was instant pleasure as the stimulation of his entry threw Annalyla over the edge and she experienced her first climax.

Somehow, the brave and honest little woman turned into a wildcat with her first coupling. Annalyla's climax had her screaming into her hand, opening her legs wider for him as he began to thrust into her in the primal ritual of mating. It was an intense experience for her as well for as him. The moment he entered her, he could feel her release, and it didn't seem to stop. Her entire body convulsed as he thrust into her repeatedly, something that drove him into the abyss of ecstasy until he released himself so hard that he bit his cheek. It was glorious. Her wet heat throbbed around him, pulling at him, milking him for his seed.

It was a powerful moment, something Tenner had never experienced in his life. Even though he'd spent himself, he couldn't stop moving within her, feeling her body contract and convulse. The more he thrust, the more she twitched and groaned, and his lips claimed hers once again. He held Annalyla's pelvis against his, his fingers in the crack of her buttocks as the moisture from his body dampened her flesh. It was mating beyond his wildest dreams and, at some point, he could feel himself grow hard again. Soon enough, another climax washed over his body as beneath him, Annalyla gasped for air. Wave after wave of rapture coursed through her.

Finally, his movements slowed and the only sound that filled the small chamber was that of Annalyla's heavy breathing. As he lay on top of her, still joined to her body, he could hardly believe what had just happened. He'd been aroused in a way he never knew possible, married to a woman who already made his blood boil.

He'd never known anything like it.

"Are you well?" he whispered.

In his embrace, he could feel her nod. "I am," she murmured.

"Are you certain?"

"Positive. May… may I say something?"

"I wish you would."

"I think you take the lead rather well."

He started to laugh, his big body shaking with mirth as he shifted his weight so he wasn't on top of her. She was a little thing and he could only imagine how uncomfortable his full weight must have been, but she didn't seem to mind. In fact, her arms were around his neck, still clinging to him, as he pulled her into a snug embrace.

"Thank you," he said, kissing her forehead. "It *was* rather marvelous."

Annalyla had nothing to compare it to, but she knew she liked it. Nay, *more* than that. She knew she could come to crave it. The warmth and the intimacy were things she could have never expected, but they were things she realized she needed – from a cold father, to a colder nurse, and from a life where she never truly belonged anywhere, to anyone, now, she finally had that sense of belonging.

To the husband she'd been dreading.

He was dreaded no more.

CHAPTER SEVEN

THEY COULD SEE it in the distance.

Outlined against the sun setting in the western sky, it was a great and dark beast of a structure. With the sky streaked with gray and orange behind it, and the great ball of golden sun half-buried on the horizon, there was nothing warm or welcoming about Baiadepaura Castle.

Even the sight of it filled the air with dread.

As Annalyla looked at the castle on the cliff, she could believe all of the tales that Graham had told her, and more. She could see the wicked lord as he did his evil deeds, and she could see the villagers with torches who had broken into his castle and burned him to death. With the great rib bones of the derelict fortress stamped against the sky, she could believe absolutely everything terrible about the place.

It was a corpse of evils past.

Around her, the five hundred Tiverton men seemed to have grown oddly silent. It had been three long days of travel from Seven Crosses because of the weather, with tempest after tempest blowing in from the west, soaking the land and then blowing away. There had been intermittent spots of clear sky, but not enough to dry out man or beast before another storm blew in and pummeled the land once more.

By the time they reached their destination, everyone was exhausted from having done battle with the elements. They were all soaked to the skin, including Annalyla. Her green woolen cloak was saturated, but the rain hadn't come through to her garments beneath because of the fur lining. She was still dry for the most part, which is more than could be said for the knights who were working the men, driving them down the muddy road as they headed for their destination. They were soaked all the way through and, in spite of the attention given by the squires who had come with the troops, their mail was starting to rust. It was leaving red marks on their necks, making it look like someone had tried to cut their throats.

"I swear to you that the men are moving more slowly," Tenner said as he reined his foaming steed next to Annalyla's little horse. "The closer we get, the slower they move."

Annalyla was getting that sense, also. She glanced at Maude next to her, seeing the woman's somewhat concerned expression.

"Graham has not been telling them any stories," she said, thinking to defend the former St. Lo knight. "I am sure he would not do that."

Tenner grunted. "He does not need to. The men know the tales. They know the rumors."

"Do you think they are afraid?"

Tenner lifted a dark eyebrow, looking over the men who were slugging through the red mud. "Let us say that they do not relish reaching our final destination," he said. "Most men are superstitious, and especially soldiers. They are like sailors in that regard – everything is an omen, and they take curses very seriously."

"They'll like it worse if we all catch our deaths out here in the dampness," Annalyla said. "We really should find decent shelter, and soon."

Tenner pursed his lips unhappily and suddenly swung his big horse about. He charged back along the line of men, shouting.

"My wife is cold and wet!" he bellowed. "If she becomes ill because you are a bunch of old women dragging your feet, then I will take it out on each and every one of you! *Move!*"

With that, the line suddenly started to pick up pace, leaving Annalyla and Maude to hide their grins as the horses began to move faster. Mud was splashing up on the horses' legs, mottling the hems of their dresses that hung down by their stirrups. Looking down at her traveling garment, Annalyla knew that it would take some cleaning to get it all out. But she was eager to reach the hulking structure of Baiadepaura Castle regardless of the fact that the men didn't seem to be, except when threatened.

In truth, she was sick of traveling. Not just from Seven Crosses, but all the way from Roseden. Annalyla hadn't stopped traveling for almost three weeks, but the leg from Seven Crosses to Baiadepaura had been different – she was traveling with Tenner now, who had been kind and attentive the entire time, and she felt as if they were embarking on a grand new adventure as husband and wife.

It was all so new and exciting, in spite of the stormy skies and endless rain. The smiles Tenner gave her along their journey kept her warm, and during the nights when they'd stopped to rest, she'd fallen asleep, safe and comfortable, in his arms. It was a joy she never knew existed, and the memories of the lies and deceit she'd brought with her had all but vanished. Those things didn't exist any longer.

Now, it was just her and Tenner.

With the quickened pace, the army from Seven Crosses reached the bulk of Baiadepaura Castle and as they drew closer, the reality of what Baiadepaura was settled deep. Viewing it from a distance was only part of it. Seeing it up close told a far more detailed tale – the place was a shell of a castle, a massive complex that stretched along the cliff, but it looked as if it had been partially dismantled.

Tenner, who was up at point along with Arlo, put out a hand to halt the column, and everyone came to a stop as Tenner and Arlo charged off through a gatehouse that was wide open. Annalyla found herself looking up at the twin cylindrical towers as they stretched to the sky.

"Look at it," she said, absorbing the sight. "I did not know it would be so…"

"Broken?" Graham had come up behind her, filling in the word she was looking for. He, too, was looking at the derelict structure. "Broken and ruined. I am not entirely sure it could be any other way."

Annalyla turned to him. "It hasn't been abandoned since the wicked lord was killed, has it?"

Graham shook his head. "Nay," he said. "I have heard that it has belonged to various Cornwall lords since that time. I think it was the Lords of Truro who built the stone walls, but you can still see the big mounds of earth around it. In ancient times, those were the original walls."

Annalyla could, indeed, see great mounds of grass-covered earth that embraced the stone walls of the castle. There was about a ten-foot gap between the berms and the walls, and there were actually two gatehouses that she could see – the big one looming before them and then a smaller one to the south. The entire shape of the castle was odd, an awkward shape due to the line of the cliff that the castle was huddled against. It was all rather fascinating but no less intimidating.

In fact, the more she looked at it, the more gloom she felt.

"It feels as if this place is a beast waiting to spring to life," Annalyla muttered, feeling a distinct sense of foreboding as the wind whistled around them. "I feel as if… as if it is watching us."

Graham grunted. "It probably is," he said. "I know I told you stories of this place, but they are just that – stories. What I see before me is a sad place that needs its dignity returned. Mayhap, that is a better way to look at it."

Annalyla wasn't so sure. She couldn't shake the sense of doom. She'd told Tenner she didn't believe any of Graham's stories. But now that she was looking at the place, she could easily believe what she'd been told.

The entire place had a dark feel to it.

As she pondered the darkness at hand, Tenner and Arlo came charging back through the gatehouse, heading straight for them. The men in the front moved aside as the knights headed for the women.

"I will have you women wait out here with a contingent of men while the rest of us clear out the place," Tenner said grimly. "It looks as if someone has been inhabiting the castle, although we didn't see anyone in a cursory check. If someone is there, then we shall flush him – or them – out."

Annalyla glanced overhead; storm clouds were starting to gather again. "Will it take long?"

Tenner shook his head. "Nay," he said, glancing up at the sky also. "Hopefully, before the rain comes again. Stay here with Graham. We shall clear the place out and make it safe for you and Maude."

Annalyla nodded, watching as Tenner and Arlo took about four hundred men with them, back through the ruined gatehouse and into what seemed to be a vast bailey. Graham gathered the remaining hundred men around the women, who ended up dismounting their horses because their backsides were aching. The ground was wet, but it was better than an aching arse. As they stretched their legs a bit, thunder rolled overhead and a swift sea breeze kicked up. Salt sprayed up the cliffs, creating clouds of mist that rose into the sky.

"My grandmother was from Kent," Maude said, moving to stand next to Annalyla and looping her arm companionably through her new friend's. "She lived in St. Margaret's, near Dover Castle. I spent time with her as a child and the smell of the sea always reminds me of her."

Annalyla turned to her. "I have spent my life in places where there was no sea," she said. "This is new to me, but there is something clean and cold and crisp about it."

Maude smiled at her. "You shall like living near the sea," she said. "This is your home now, even though it looks as if giants have kicked it over like a great sand pile. I am looking forward to walking the beaches with you and collecting shells."

That sounded rather pleasant, in distinct contrast to the gloom Annalyla felt about the place. Was it possible that there was actually some light to this dark and unholy place? She opened her mouth to reply, but the sounds of distant shouting shook them from their conversation. Soon, they heard the thunder of horses. They turned to see men coming from the smaller gatehouse to the south, as well as from the main gatehouse, in an action suggesting that at least some of the castle had been secured.

Above, more thunder rolled and Graham dismounted his horse to help the ladies back onto their palfreys. By the time Maude was mounted and gathering her reins, Tenner was coming from the main gatehouse, bringing up the rear of his men. His charger was kicking up mud and clumps of earth as he once again headed towards the women. Only this time, he lifted an arm and began to wave it towards the castle.

"Move the men," he called to Graham. Then, he turned to the women. "Come along, ladies. Let us get into shelter before this storm lets loose."

"Is it safe?" Annalyla called to him.

He nodded, struggling with his excitable steed. "Safe enough," he told her. "Come along, Lady de Velt."

Everyone began rushing towards the main gatehouse as the first big drops of rain began to fall. The thunder was deafening as lightning streaked across the sky. Annalyla didn't see much of the gatehouse as they quickly passed through it, but she could certainly smell it – it smelled of puddles of rancid water. But once they were into the vast bailey, she could finally see the castle for what it was –

A skeleton.

Lightning lit up the sky again and she could see the keep directly in front of her. It was a keep unlike anything she'd ever seen before – there was a big, square box of a building in the center with two wings on either side. Part of the north wing was collapsed on the top floor, but the south wing seemed intact, and the central part of the keep also seemed relatively undamaged.

The rain began to fall harder as Tenner pulled her off the palfrey and guided her towards a large building that was built against the outer wall. At one time, it had a double-door entry, but one door was missing while the other was warped. As he pulled her into the structure, she could see that it was the great hall.

It was a vast, decomposing chamber, partially filling with smoke as men went about building a fire in the center of the hall, in a fire pit like the old Saxon halls had. Smoke would rise to the ceiling and find outlets through holes in the roof. But in this case, a corner of the roof was missing and rain was coming through, mixing with the smoke to drive it back inward. Tenner had a grip on her as they walked towards the fire pit.

"Unfortunately, the entire place is like this," he grumbled. "Crumbling and derelict. From what I have seen, the hall is the best place for you and Maude at the moment, so remain here while we secure the place."

He let her go and turned away, but Annalyla grasped his arm. "Did you find anyone living here?"

Tenner shook his head, his cheeks marked red by the mail that was rusting around his head. "Nay," he replied, "but there are signs that someone has been living here recently. There are animal carcasses, fish bones, that kind of thing. There is rubbish all around, just like the rest of this place. Purely rubbish."

Annalyla sensed that he was greatly annoyed by the situation and she suspected why. He'd spoken proudly of his new garrison but to see the reality of it had somewhat damaged his pride. He'd been given a pile of old stones to govern. Rubbish, as he called it. Taking his hand, Annalyla smiled encouragingly at him.

"Do not fret," she said. "It has been unattended for quite some time, but now that you are here, it will shine again. You will see to it. With a de Velt in command, perfection is assured."

He stared at her a moment before breaking down into a weak smile. "And how would you know that?"

She laughed softly. "I grew up in the north, where de Velt reigns," she said. "I know what men say about the battle lords of de Velt. And I know that you will make this a mighty outpost, so do not be discouraged by what you see. Tomorrow, you will assess the situation and make plans accordingly. You will turn this place into a great fortress."

Tenner was softened by her words. It was true that he was discouraged by what he saw; it was difficult not to be. He'd come into possession of a rotting pile of stones rather than the mighty castle he'd hoped for. It was true that it was a place with a dark reputation, but he had hoped it had at least been kept up and maintained over the years by the string of owners it had belonged to.

Yet it was clear that was not the case; Baiadepaura was in ruins. He had quite a task on his hands, on top of the fact that he'd never wanted to bring women here in the first place. He had no way to protect them without gates and doors, or even the slightest measure of security, and that greatly disturbed him. Looking into Annalyla's lovely face, the sense of protection he felt towards her was almost more than he could bear.

His wife...

The woman he never wanted, yet the woman that, in two days, had somehow embedded herself under his skin. They hadn't spent much time together, except to sleep and the occasional meal, but in those brief moments he'd come to see a woman of wit and humor. Bit by bit, he was coming to know her and liking what he saw. He was coming to understand her a little and she, in turn, was coming to understand him. This was a perfect example. She knew their arrival had disappointed him and she was trying to give him some comfort. Even in the short time they'd known one another, already, she was sensing his moods.

He'd never had anyone care enough to do that.

"Your confidence in me is appreciated," he said, reaching up to touch her cheek with a gloved finger in a gesture of genuine affection. "To be honest, the state of the castle does not upset me as much as the lack of security for you and Maude does. It is safer if you remain here in the hall with soldiers to protect you. I intend to inspect the keep from top to bottom and see if it will be suitable for us to sleep in tonight. Given the state of the entire place, I am not holding out hope."

She grinned. "You *could* be surprised."

"I doubt it."

With a wink, he left her, heading out into the storm that was now beginning to rage. Annalyla stood there, her heart fluttering as she watched him go, before turning to look around the hall, watching the rain come in through the leaking roof.

"It's quite a mess," Maude said.

She turned to the woman, who was standing near the fire trying to dry out her clothing. Steam was rising as it heated the wet fabric.

"Aye," Annalyla agreed, taking a few steps towards the fire and lifting her wet hands. "I feel terrible for Tenner. He seems so disappointed."

Maude peeled off her gloves, wringing them out. "He will forget about it," she said. "The thrill of his first command will have him forgetting any disappointment. Now, it seems as if we must get a few things in order while the men complete their tasks. What would you have me do, Lady de Velt?"

As she said it, Annalyla realized that she was now the chatelaine of this place, broken down as it was. Still, it was hers, and the thrill of that realization filled her with excitement. Looking around the dilapidated hall, it suddenly didn't look so terrible to her. It was still dark and the gloom she felt hadn't lifted, but that was of little matter. As she had told Tenner, it was a place he could make shine again, and so could she. They would do it together. When she thought of it that way, it was the most beautiful place she'd ever seen.

It was time to roll up her sleeves and get busy.

"Indeed," she said after a moment. "I would say that the first order of business is feeding the men, wouldn't you? Where is the quartermaster? We need his supplies."

Maude cast her an approving smile before heading back towards the entry where soldiers were coming in out of the rain. Annalyla could hear Maude speaking to them, asking about the quartermaster, but she didn't hear much of the ensuing conversation. At that point, she was on her own quest. If they were going to cook a meal, then they would need something to cook it with. Seeing Graham as he organized men near the smaller servant door, she called out to the man.

"Graham!" she said. When he looked at her, she waved him over. "To me!"

The knight obediently went to her. "My lady?"

"I need something to cook with," she said. "I am assuming that the quartermaster will be feeding the army?"

Graham nodded. "That is usual," he eyed her. "Why do you need something to cook with?"

"Because I wish to prepare hot food for the knights. I want to see what the quartermaster has so that I can prepare food. I need the pots to do it in."

Graham lifted a dubious eyebrow. "Forgive me, my lady, but do you even know how to prepare a meal? That is servants' work."

She knew that. "That is true, but you know that in the absence of my mother, I was chatelaine at Roseden," she said patiently. "I may not have been the cook, but I have overseen numerous meals. Surely I know enough to prepare something quite competently, so find me any iron pots that you can. There must be something around here, especially if someone has recently been inhabiting the place, as my husband said."

Graham wasn't exactly sure it was a good idea for Annalyla to cook something, but he didn't argue with her. She would do what she damn well pleased, anyway. He simply nodded his head and turned away, heading back towards the servant's entrance to the hall.

Annalyla watched him lumber off, knowing he didn't approve of what she was doing. But like a good servant, he did as he was told. As she watched him giving instructions to some of the soldiers at the door, she turned to see Maude heading in her direction with the quartermaster, a man she'd seen for the past couple of days but hadn't really spoken with. All she knew was that he fed the men on a good deal of bread and little else. She went to meet them.

"My lady," the quartermaster greeted her. A man with a crown of wild white hair, he had a round face and a red nose, pinched with the cold. "Lady de Correa says that you wish to know what supplies I have?"

Annalyla nodded. "I do," she said. "And I am curious why you have been feeding the men so heavily on bread the past two days. Old bread, too. It was baked at Seven Crosses."

The old man nodded. "Aye, my lady," he said. "It was. I find that men travel better on bread. It weighs heavily in the stomach and gives them strength for the long march."

"True, but it does not keep their hunger sated for very long," she said. "What meat provisions have you brought?"

The man gestured back to the wagon, which had been pulled up right outside the hall door. "I have barrels of salted beef, my lady," he said. "I also have some salt pork, wheat flour, oats, cheese, eggs, apples, onions, carrots, cabbage, salt, and I brought along some spices in case the meat turned sour."

Annalyla thought on that. "How long will those supplies last?"

"I've brought enough for the men to eat for at least a week, my lady," he said. "We can catch fish in the sea, or hunt for our meat in the local forests. I've also heard that there is a market in Widemouth."

Annalyla lifted her eyebrows. "The forests may belong to the king," she said. "We cannot hunt there if that is the case."

"I doubt the king will know, my lady."

It sounded risky to her and she was certain Tenner would think the same thing, but she didn't say so. Instead, she turned to Maude.

"We are going to have to purchase some supplies until we can get the kitchens running," she said. "We'll need chickens, and a milk cow and calf. We did not bring any of that with us, and we will need those items. I do not wish to bother my husband about these things; he has enough to worry about with this derelict old place. If we can have him assign us a few men, then we can send them out looking for cattle to purchase. There may even be a farm nearby where we can purchase cheese and butter to fortify our stores."

Maude was smiling at her as she spoke. "You sound very much as if you know what you are doing," she said. "You said that your father's castle wasn't nearly the size of Seven Crosses, but that does not diminish your knowledge in what should be done. I agree with everything you have said."

Annalyla smiled, rather embarrassed. "I do not sound like a tyrant, do I?"

"Very much so. But that is what this place needs."

Annalyla laughed softly. "Then you and I are of one mindset," she said. "Tomorrow, we shall put our plan into action. But for now, we have men to feed."

"Indeed."

Annalyla returned her attention to the quartermaster. "Bring in the supplies," she said. "Bring in all of them and stack them over there against the wall. Bring in whatever pots you have, because the men are going to eat well tonight."

The quartermaster nodded, somewhat nervously. In just the short conversation he'd had with her, he could see that Lady de Velt was a strong-willed woman.

"Aye, my lady," he said. "What would you have them eat?"

Annalyla pondered that a moment. "Do you have cooking pots?"

"Big ones, my lady."

"Then fill them with water and bring them in here," she said. "Boil the beef and boil the carrots. If we can find some flattened rocks or stone, we can heat them up in the fire and bake bread on them. Can you do that?"

The man nodded firmly. "Aye, my lady."

"Good," Annalyla said. "Have men help you bring in the supplies while Lady de Correa and I organize everything. Hurry, now, the men are hungry."

The quartermaster fled, grabbing a few men as he went. They headed out into the storm and, soon enough, barrels of beef and sacks of precious foodstuffs were brought back into the hall as Maude directed the men to stack everything up against the dry eastern wall so they could get an accounting of everything.

More and more men began filtering outside, returning with their arms full of things. When Annalyla saw the pots coming in, she grabbed a couple, including a few iron pans, with sides that were an inch or two high, that were used for baked dishes. Bowls and spoons and other implements were brought in, organized by Maude and Annalyla themselves. And in no time, the old quartermaster was well on his way to boiling beef for the men as Annalyla and Maude planned a different menu for the knights.

Considering that the most either of them had done was watch the cooks prepare meals, they were good with their educated guesses. Into one of the pots that Annalyla had confiscated went heads of cabbage, torn up because she didn't have a knife, and chunks of broken carrots. Enough water was added to fill the pot about two-thirds full. Onions and turnips proved more difficult to break up with their hands, so Maude borrowed a sharp dagger from one of the soldiers and used it to cut up the root vegetables, tossing them into the cabbage mixture along with a piece of salt pork. Placing the pot on the edge of the fire ensured that it would soon be bubbling. Annalyla added a little more salt and powdered mustard, and stirred it all up.

With the cabbage potage on the fire, they moved to the eggs. They had four iron baking dishes and Annalyla made a dough from the wheat flour, a little water, salt, an egg yolk, and some lard. She had seen the cook at Roseden do it, and although she didn't know the exact measurements, she guessed at what she could recall. She hoped it was right. Once the dough had been pressed into the baking dishes to form a crust, she beat the eggs in a bowl with more cut up onions, and bits of tart, white cheese that Maude had put into it, and poured the mixture into the four baking dishes. Sprinkling the coarse salt over the top of it, she set the dishes next to the steaming pot so that the eggs could bake.

When that was done, Annalyla and Maude sat back to observe their handiwork. There was nothing left to do now but wait for things to bake and bubble, so they looked at each other and shrugged.

"You seem to know a good deal about food preparation," Maude said. "These dishes look delicious."

Annalyla exhaled in a slow, deliberate gesture. "I only know what I have seen others do," she admitted. "If these do not turn out, then I shall have failed spectacularly. But at least I will have tried."

"I am certain Tenner will appreciate it a great deal."

"He will until he tastes it."

They giggled at each other before gradually noticing that the quartermaster had two very large bowls of bread dough. The man was beating at the dough, kneading it, and then setting the bowls near the fire for the dough to rise. As he waddled off to do something else, Annalyla pointed at the dough.

"Let us find some clean stones and put them in the fire," she whispered loudly. "We can steal some of his dough and make bread for our husbands. I shall get the stones; *you* get the dough."

Maude nodded confidently, inching towards the dough bowls as Annalyla made her way back towards the smaller hall entry where several soldiers were gathered around, making sure to protect the entry. They didn't stop Annalyla from passing through the door, but they followed her, and she told them what she was looking for. Soon enough, she had three wet and relatively clean stones, which the men carried back into the hall for her and even put them on the fire near the steaming pot of cabbage that was beginning to smell rather good.

Once the stones were dry and heating up, Annalyla and Maude formed loaves of bread with the stolen dough and put them upon the stones, watching them immediately start to firm up.

There was a satisfaction in a task well done. They'd taken on the challenge of cooking themselves and, so far, the results seemed to be acceptable. It looked and smelled good enough. Annalyla looked at Maude with a smile on her lips, and the woman grinned and put her arm around Annalyla's shoulders as they watched their meal take shape. As Annalyla had said, it would either be a success or a spectacular failure. But at least they were willing to try, and it had been a bonding experience between them.

For the first time since leaving Netherghyll, Annalyla felt as if she were part of something, as if she had made a friend. Her time at Netherghyll had been so precious to her, and the years of heartbreak and boredom after returning to Roseden seemed like a bitter memory. All of it, a bitter memory. Now, she was where she wanted to be, where she belonged, in the hall of a derelict castle, married to a man she was coming to adore more and more by the day, and with a companion in Maude that was more, and better, than she could have ever hoped for. Perhaps, in some way, God was rewarding her for all of those years she had spent with a selfish father and a manipulative nurse.

She could only hope.

Resting her head on Maude's shoulder, the two of them watched their meal cook well into the night.

Chapter Eight

THE STORM WAS starting to lift a little as the wind blew the clouds inland. The moon, sitting in the sky above the turbulent sea, cast ghostly rays into the water in intermittent flashes as the clouds moved.

Tenner had been watching the sky from time to time as he moved about the keep, checking rooms and checking the roof, ceilings, and floor. He hadn't found any warm bodies yet, but there were definite signs of habitation in some of the rooms. At one point, he ended up on the lower floor, in a rather large room with windows that overlooked the bailey. He could see nearly the entire ward from the chamber, including the great hall, where the fire from the pit was casting a golden glow from the windows and broken doorways. He thought he could even smell baking bread.

His hall.

All of this was his. His and Annalyla's. He found himself eager to return to his wife, who was somewhere in that glowing hall, but he had a task to complete first. Baiadepaura seemed to have a maze of chambers, smaller chambers, stairwells, and even a hidden door he'd found in a wall when he'd accidentally leaned on it. He'd nearly toppled over. It was all quite fascinating, but it was also quite eerie. Inspecting an old castle that had rumors of a ghost attached to it made it so. He still didn't believe in ghosts. But looking at a place like this, he could almost believe.

Almost…

Coming out of the big chamber that overlooked the bailey, he ended up in another chamber that had windows facing out over the sea. It was still raining for the most part, and he could see a mist rolling in from the southwest. Soon, it would cover everything and they would no longer see the moon or the storm clouds high above. Everything would be shrouded in that heavy Cornwall mist. With thoughts of the coming fog on his mind, he was about to exit the chamber when a dark figure emerged into the room, startling him. Instinctively, he put his hand to the hilt of his broadsword, but the darkened figure lifted its hands in supplication.

"Easy." It was Arlo. "Did you think it was the Devil of Baiadepaura creeping up on you, then?"

Tenner had to admit his heart had jumped a little. "God only knows in this place," he muttered. "Well? What is your report from the south wing?"

Arlo stepped forward, the faint light from the fading moon on his features. "It is oddly solid," he said. "It is clear that someone has kept that part of the keep in repair, because the roof is good and so are the floors. The hearth has even been used recently."

Tenner was interested. "Is that so?"

Arlo nodded. "Aye," he said. "And there is something more, Ten. There are oil lamps in the chamber on the top floor facing south, the one with the big window that overlooks the sea. There is a path from the beach below up the slope and into the bailey; I could see it from the window."

Tenner lifted a dark eyebrow. "Lamps?" he repeated. "For signaling ships at sea, mayhap?"

Arlo nodded. "And a path for men to travel when they beach their boats. A well-used path."

Tenner could instantly see where the man was leading. "Signaling ships at sea," he muttered. "And a hidden cove. I saw that cove from the window in the next chamber over, but only part of it. You cannot see it unless you are looking right down upon it."

"That is true."

"Pirates would use a cove like that."

"And the path to a derelict castle, mayhap to hide their ill-gotten gains."

"Or even wait for other ships to pass so they can sail out to attack them."

Arlo sighed heavily. "My thoughts, exactly," he said. "I think this place has been a haven for those who have attacked Lord Tiverton's vessels from Bude and Widemouth. God only knows how long it has been abandoned, and it is a perfect place for the pirates to hide. All they have to do is sit here and wait for ships passing to the south, and because the cove is hidden, no one would see them until it was too late."

Tenner wasn't surprised to hear any of this, but he was concerned. "And now, there are five hundred men occupying this space, which will make it difficult for the pirates to reclaim it," he said. "I would say that the first thing we need to do is destroy that path from the beach to the bailey. We must make it so they cannot come up from the cove."

Arlo nodded. "Hopefully the weather will clear on the morrow and we can see what needs to be done," he said. "For tonight, however, I would suggest putting about fifty men at the trailhead, watching the cove and the seas. And, Ten… you're not going to like this."

"Like *what*?"

Arlo paused a moment. "When a squall passed through and the weather eased, I thought I saw a light out to sea."

Tenner knew exactly what he meant. "A passing ship."

"Exactly. We do not know for certain that it is a pirate ship, but…"

"But who would be traveling in this weather if it was not a predator?"

"Those are my thoughts."

Tenner grunted sharply. "Damn," he hissed. "If that is the case, then we light up this keep. Put a man in every window facing the sea and give them a lamp. They are to remain there all night. We do not need the pirates bringing their ship into the cove because they think Baiadepaura is vacant. I want no surprises this night."

"Agreed."

"And you and I and de Lave will take the night watch. Every inch of this place will be covered with men and weapons."

"Aye."

With that, they headed out of the keep and back to the great hall, which was warm and fragrant when they entered. Tenner was still on edge, still thinking about pirates, but when he saw Annalyla's face, all of that changed.

All he felt was comfort.

He found himself looking forward to sitting with her, and talking to her, if only for a few short moments before he set posts for the night. His sweet little wife who was starting to consume him. While Arlo went to find Graham and relay the orders, Tenner went straight to Annalyla, who was very proud to show him the bread she'd baked and the egg dishes that were golden-brown on the top. Tenner looked at the food in surprise.

"You did this?" he asked her. "*All* of this?"

Annalyla indicated Maude. "Maude and I did it together," she said. "We wanted to make hot food for you and Arlo. We have supervised enough meals that I think that practically makes us cooks, so I hope it turns out well. Do you have time to eat now?"

Even if Tenner didn't have time, he was going to make time. He looked at Annalyla, her cheeks flushed rosy because she'd spent so much time close to the fire, and the fact that she did this for him threatened to turn him into a giddy, smiling fool. He was very touched.

"You really did all of this yourself?" he asked. "For me?"

She grinned. "For you."

Planting himself on the ground next to the fire, he took the egg dish and, using a spoon Annalyla gave him, began to shovel great bites of egg and onion and cheese into his mouth. He quickly realized that it was salty and delicious, so he gobbled it down because he was very hungry. Next came bread, which was a little oddly-shaped because it had been baked on the stone, but it was very tasty when he dipped it into the cabbage potage that was full of onions and carrots and turnips.

Once the egg dishes were devoured, the same iron pans held the cabbage potage, and Annalyla watched Tenner eat three bowls of the stuff. Oddly, she wasn't hungry herself. She was far more interested in watching Tenner eat and she felt as if she'd accomplished something by feeding him, small as it was. To her, it was showing the man that she had some worth, that she would make a good wife as well as a good chatelaine for his new garrison. She wanted to show him that she would always take care of him, no matter what, and she wanted to make him proud.

And proud, he was.

When the meal was finished, Tenner kissed his wife and thanked her for the meal. By this time, the heavy fog had rolled in from the sea, creating a thick soup outside, so Tenner gathered his men and they headed into the fog, moving for their posts. Fifty men were left inside the hall, guarding both entrances, but Annalyla and Maude remained by the fire, eating what was left after Tenner and Arlo had eaten their fill. When the food was finished off, the women bedded down by the fire. It was warm and cozy, even though they were sleeping on the hard-packed earth.

But for Annalyla, it didn't matter. She was home now, in that dark and crumbling castle by the sea. The meal and the warm fire had soothed any eeriness she had about the place, and she was looking forward to the morning and seeing the entire building for herself. Things, for the moment, were pleasant, and she was quite weary from the journey. Just as she began to close her eyes and settle down for sleep, a mournful wail could be heard over the castle grounds, something that seemed to sweep from one side to the other. They could hear it moving from the north to the south, only to fade away into the fog as if drifting off to sea.

For a moment, no one moved. Perhaps it was fear that kept them still, or perhaps it was shock. In any case, no one dared more for a moment until Annalyla's head slowly lifted.

"What… what was that?" she whispered.

Maude sat up beside her, looking to the main entry where the soldiers seemed to be on edge. "I do not know," she said, feeling some of that fear that Annalyla had been feeling about the place since nearly the beginning. "But do not worry, Annie. We are well protected. The soldiers will not allow us to be harmed. Go to sleep now."

Annalyla wasn't sure she could, but she lay back down again, with Maude's hand on her shoulder. Together, they lay there, each of them pretending to sleep but unable to do so. The cry they'd all heard had been unsettling at best.

Perhaps it had been the ghost of Baiadepaura they'd all heard tale of.

Perhaps the rumors had, in fact, been true.

It was a terrifying thought. When Annalyla finally drifted off, it was with dreams of wicked lords and crumbling castles.

CHAPTER NINE

10 miles north of Widemouth Bay
The Bleeding Saint Inn, the village of St. Morwenna

"BY ALL THE Gods, the mist is thick this night."

It was a decidedly Scottish accent that filled the stale air of the stale inn, a tavern packed with bodies, with people who had come in out of the foul weather seeking shelter and a bit of warmth against the fog that had descended on this night.

But there was no warmth to be found.

As crowded as it was, more men were coming in, looking for any corner to hide in as if fleeing from the mist that had cloaked the land, clinging to everything in the wake of a rainstorm that had blown off to the east.

Following the dregs and street urchins, men clad in leather and woolens, with weapons and the smell of the sea about them, entered the inn and commandeered a table near the door, isolating themselves from the rest of the population of the inn.

These men had come with a purpose.

The first purpose was to drink and, perhaps, find a warm meal. Their vessel, the *Beast of the Seas*, was part of the greater pirate faction of Scottish pirates. Based on the Isle of Scarba in the Highlands of Scotland, they roamed the western coasts of Scotland, Ireland, and England, and often ventured to the eastern coast of Ireland if they were feeling particularly aggressive. They took what they wanted, claimed without fear, and dared men to challenge them.

Such was their nature.

For the past three years, the Cornwall coast had been their feeding ground. From St. Ives all the way north to Barnstaple, they'd claimed that particular stretch of coast as their own and woe betide the ships that passed through their domain. The *Beast of the Seas* was a fast ship, a modified cog stolen from the hated French pirates, and it could easily overtake the slower merchant cogs that traveled south and around the tip of Cornwall on their journey eastward.

But for their pirating purposes, they also needed land bases, coves, and beaches that they could secure the ship in while waiting for their prey. They had such a place just north of St. Ives and then another one further up the coast at Holywell, where there was a massive sea cave that, at low tide, they could use to completely shield the ship. They had to be careful near Tintagel Castle because the Earl of Cornwall kept troops there, troops who had a ship of their own to sail out and intercept the pirates if they had a mind to, which they sometimes did.

Therefore, Tintagel was mostly avoided, but further north was the hulking shell of Baiadepaura Castle that had both a secluded beach and a land-based structure in the abandoned castle itself, where the pirates could gather more men or hide their ill-gotten gains. They'd been using Baiadepaura for the past three years and had taken great pride in it. But tonight, that had changed.

The abandoned castle was no longer abandoned.

There had been lights in the windows of the keep, shining out to sea, as the pirates had noticed whilst sailing north. Worse still, there were men all around the place, from what they had seen. It had been difficult to see much considering the storm and the decreased visibility, but with his spyglass, Captain Raleigh "Leigh" MacBeth had seen the lights and the dark figures that represented men. Somehow, someway, the legend of Baiadepaura failed to keep away some brave souls who had foolishly thought to inhabit what the pirates claimed as their own.

But that would be their undoing.

"I wouldna worry about the mist," Raleigh spoke to the man who had lamented about the fog. "We have bigger issues than that, laddie."

The heads around the table bobbed to varying degrees as his men agreed with him. There were eight men around the table total, with the rest of the crew remaining on the *Beast of the Seas* because someone had to man the ship and remain vigilant to anything happening upon the stormy sea this night.

Therefore, the men that had come to the inn were the heart of the command crew, hardened men who could kill as easily as breathe, steal as easily as smile. It was all second nature to them, for life upon the seas was brutal as well as difficult. It could age a man before his time. Raleigh looked around the table at his assorted crew of misfits.

"So the Bay of Fear is no longer empty," he said after a moment. "I must say that I'm surprised tae see that. I thought no one but a madman would go near that terrible place."

His men chuckled, just a little. "*We* have," one of the men said, an older sea dog with a weathered face. "'Twas a perfect nest for us scavengers."

More low laughter. "Ye said no one wanted it," another man said. "Ye said it was a wicked place, too wicked for reasonable men."

Raleigh lifted his shoulders. "It belongs tae someone," he said. "The Earl of Cornwall, I last heard, but he keeps no men there. Even he knows of the evil of that place."

"Then he's changed his mind," the same man said. "Now, there are men there, men who have undoubtedly seen evidence that someone else has been living there."

"But we've left nothing behind." A third man spoke up, the same man who had commented on the mist when they'd first entered the inn. "We moved what booty we kept there a few days ago. There's nothing left."

Raleigh turned to the man. Alastair MacMurdoc was a good man and an even better pirate, but he tended to complain like an old woman at times.

"Nay, there's nothing left," Raleigh agreed. "But Baiadepaura has been vacant for years. We claimed it three years ago and since that time, it has belonged only tae us. I want it back."

A serving wench with a red nose and a wet cough brought a pitcher of ale, a pitcher of wine, and cups, setting them on the table as the men swooped in on the alcohol. They were thirsty. She eyed Alastair because she knew the man, and she was hoping for a bit of fun from him, but he shoved her away. He had no time for the runny-nosed wench this night. He was far more concerned with Raleigh's statement.

"We dunna know how many men are there," he said after the wench left. "We dunna know if 'tis the Earl of Cornwall, and if he's brought his whole army."

That wasn't what Raleigh wanted to hear. He couldn't stomach the tone of defeat already in Alastair's voice.

"I'll not tolerate yer cowardice, Alastair," he growled. "We need Baiadepaura. The place has been vacant for three long years and do ye know why? Because of the ghost that roams the place. We've all seen it."

Pirates were a superstitious bunch. It seemed odd that they would inhabit a haunted castle. But the truth was that they tolerated it because, for their purposes, the location was perfect. Men would stay away from Baiadepaura because of the legend, allowing them to conduct their illicit business.

Still, at the mention of the ghost, they eyed each other, nodding as if fearful to even admit such a thing. Admitting it was acknowledging that they'd all seen a curse in action, and no one wanted to do that.

Curses could kill.

"Aye, we've seen it," Alastair said. "We've seen it and we've run from it. I dunna know one man here who hasna run from it. Few of us will stay in the keep after dark, Leigh."

Raleigh pointed a finger at him. "Exactly," he said. "And the men at Baiadepaura now will see that ghost and they will run. But we canna wait for that tae happen."

"What do ye mean?"

Raleigh downed the warmed, cheap wine in his cup. "Baiadepaura has a ghost," he said. "We know that. But mayhap, we give the ghost a little help by becoming ghosts ourselves. What man can stay at a place that is full of a company of ghosts?"

Alastair looked at him with doubt. "So we pretend we are phantoms and chase them away?"

Raleigh nodded vigorously. "The sooner the better. Ye know the fat merchant vessel from Plymouth is due in these waters in the next few days, the one that comes this time every year headed for Dublin. We need Baiadepaura if we are tae take the ship and her goods."

Alastair thought it was a rather ridiculous plan – pretending to be ghosts. He sat forward, his eyes glittering in the weak light of the inn.

"I have a better idea," he said. "Old Mawgwen lives in Bude. Ye remember the woman. She works at The Sea and The Siren, the tavern near the edge of town."

"The old wench who tells the fortunes?"

"The same," Alastair continued. "Ye know her people have lived and worked at Baiadepaura for centuries back. If anyone knows of the place, 'tis her. We could send her tae Baiadepaura with her terrible tales and they couldna ignore a woman whose family is part of the legend of the castle. If she tells them tae leave, then mayhap they'd listen tae her."

"And if they dunna?"

He shrugged. "Then we know Baiadepaura. We know how tae get in and out of the place. If there is an army at Baiadepaura, then there are commanders. If old Mawgwen canna force them tae leave with her stories, then we kill the commanders. What men are left will surely flee. Blame that on the ghosts, and the truth of Mawgwen's tales, but I say we take that action instead of pretending tae be phantoms."

Raleigh had poured himself more wine and was in the process of downing the second cup. "Ye could be right, laddie," he said, licking his lips. "Let old Mawgwen give it a try. If it doesna work, then a few of us will go in and remove those in command. A headless army will be helpless, especially if they believe the curse of Baiadepaura is responsible for the deaths. 'Twill be the curse in action for all they know."

"When do ye think tae move on Baiadepaura?"

Raleigh continued smacking his lips of the bitter wine. "Tomorrow night," he said firmly. "We can sail back down the coast tae Bude and tell Mawgwen we have a task for her. Then, we continue down the coast tae Crackington Cove, south of Baiadepaura, where we can hide the ship. We'll travel on foot tae the castle and watch. If we see the army leaving by nightfall, then we wait for them tae leave. But if they dunna leave…"

"Then we take matters intae our own hands."

The more the men around the table drank, the more Raleigh's plan seemed to make some sense. They were incensed that the ruins of Baiadepaura had been invaded, because the place had been a perfect base for the thievery on the high seas. As they began to mutter amongst themselves, in agreement with Raleigh's plans, Alastair turned to his captain.

"'Tis the right idea tae bring the curse tae life," he said, lowering his voice.

Raleigh's dark eyes glittered. "If the real phantom doesna chase them away first. One can always hope."

Alastair wasn't hard pressed to agree. He poured himself more wine. "But one canna summon the Devil of Baiadepaura," he said. "The Devil appears when he wishes. We canna depend upon it."

Raleigh nodded. "Which is why we're going tae give the ghost some help," he said, lifting his cup to his second in command. "Here's tae regaining Baiadepaura. I want my castle back."

Alastair lifted his cup in return. "Here's tae the curse that all men fear."

Raleigh cocked a bushy red eyebrow. "If the men that occupy Baiadepaura dunna fear it yet, by tomorrow night, they will. I promise ye."

Alastair had no doubt. What Raleigh MacBeth wanted, Raleigh MacBeth got.

Tomorrow night, he would have it.

CHAPTER TEN

Baiadepaura Castle

ANNALYLA AWOKE TO someone gently shaking her.

"Annalyla?" came the soft whisper. "Wake up, sweetheart."

Annalyla resisted. She could hear the voice, a soft male voice, but she ignored it. She was so exhausted that she simply couldn't open her eyes, but then she heard a female voice in her other ear.

"Annie, wake up. The day is new and we have much work to do. Get up!"

Annalyla's eyes flew open at the sound of Maude's stern voice. When she saw both Tenner and Maude looking down at her, she sat up so quickly that she nearly hit Tenner in the jaw. He laughed softly as she struggled to catch her balance.

"Easy, lass," he said, his hands on her shoulders to steady her. "There is nothing to panic over. You were sleeping so peacefully that we did not want to wake you, but it was necessary. I am afraid that it is our first day in our new home and I need your assistance."

Annalyla stifled a yawn. "I am honored to assist you," she said. "What can I do?"

Tenner was snorting at her, half-asleep even though she pretended not to be. She was blinking her eyes, pretending to be instantly wide awake. But he could tell she wasn't. He cupped her face between his big palms and kissed her on the forehead.

"You can help me assess the keep once you have fully awakened," he said. "Unless you plan to sleep in the great hall forever, then I suggest we find chambers that please you. Maude will see to the morning meal if you will accompany me."

Annalyla stifled another yawn, but she nodded her head. "I would be happy to," she said. "May I at least comb my hair first?"

Tenner was smiling at her as he stood up. "Of course, you may," he said. "Your baggage has been brought in. May I bring you what you need?"

It was a sweet offer and his eyes were twinkling at her as he said it. Annalyla gazed up at him, her heart never fuller than it was at that moment. Every day saw the man grow more attentive and, perhaps, even kinder, if such a thing was possible. But as she looked at him, she realized that he looked rather exhausted. His hair was hanging over the right side of his face as it always did, exposing the left eye, which had a dark circle beneath it.

"Did you sleep at all last night, Tenner?" she asked. "You look weary."

The smile never left his face. "I took the night watch, along with every man here," he said. "Our first night in a place with no walls and no gates, I could not sleep. But I am glad you did. That means I did my job; you felt safe enough to sleep."

Annalyla nodded her head, smiling gratefully at Maude when the woman handed her a cup of warmed, watered wine.

"You have done so much while I slept the morning away," she said, looking between Maude and Tenner. "I am ashamed I slept through everything."

As Tenner headed for the baggage that had been stacked against a dry wall, Maude took charge of Annalyla's hair, which was sticking up like straw.

"You were very tired," Maude said. "You have been traveling far more than the rest of us, since you came all the way from the north. You have earned a good rest. I am sorry I had to wake you when I did."

Annalyla reached back to pat at the woman's hand in a gesture of thanks, of perhaps comfort, as Maude proceeded to unbraid her messy hair. As Annalyla sipped at her warmed wine, Maude dug around in the satchel that Tenner brought over and found a comb. She proceeded to comb out Annalyla's blonde hair and re-braid it securely.

All the while, Annalyla sipped at her wine, trying to wake up, and watched Tenner as the man moved around the hall, speaking to some of the soldiers, and speaking to Graham and Arlo, who had come in and out of the smaller servant door to the south. They all looked weary, having been up all night, but she couldn't take her eyes off of Tenner.

Tall, strong, proud...

There wasn't anything about the man that was imperfect, from the top of his dark head to the bottom of his big feet. He handled men with ease, with a quiet confidence that was both reassuring and respectful. Maude was tugging on her hair, and she was sipping the hot wine, which burned her tongue, but none of that even registered with her. All that mattered was the knight with the shoulder-length hair, hanging down over the right side of his face.

It occurred to Annalyla that she didn't like the fact that he was covering up that handsome face. He let his hair fall over his dual-colored eye and she was coming to realize that he did it on purpose; he'd been doing it since the moment they'd met. When he finished speaking to Arlo and sent the man on his way, she caught his attention and crooked a finger at him. The smile returned to his lips as he headed in her direction.

"My lady?" he asked politely.

Annalyla didn't say anything. She crooked her finger again so that he would come down to her level. He did, taking a knee in front of her, and she reached up, pushing the hair away from the right side of his face.

"There," she said softly. "Now I can see all of you."

He blinked at her, uncertain, and feeling instantly self-conscious now that his right eye was exposed. The smile on his lips turned into something of a grimace.

"I… I do not know what you mean," he said. "You always see all of me."

It was her turn to smile. "Do you think the eye with green in it is in any way unappealing to me?" she asked. "I told you when I met you that your sister has the same eyes. I find them striking and enchanting. Please do not hide it from me. It is handsome, as is the rest of you."

He stared at her a moment and Annalyla swore she saw the man blush. In fact, he averted his gaze, unsure what to say to her, but she put a soft hand on his cheek and patted him sweetly. In spite of the natural embarrassment he was feeling when it came to his eye, he chuckled at her. He wasn't sure how to react other than that.

"Do you wish me to cut my hair off, then?" he asked. "So it does not hang in my face? It has always done that, since I was a lad."

She cocked an eyebrow. "I think it has always done that because someone told you once that your eye was disturbing," she said. "I cannot imagine that unique feature has not gone unnoticed by others."

He shook his head, his smile fading. "It has not."

"I think it is quite attractive. You need not hide it from me, but I will not force you to keep it uncovered if you do not wish to."

He simply looked at her, at a loss for words. Of course, he was self-conscious of the eye. He had been for as long as he could recall, so covering it with his hair was second nature. Annalyla was the first person, other than his mother, to tell him that his two-colored eyes were something unique and beautiful. Tenner never thought he'd find a woman who could look past the oddity of it, or the darkness of the de Velt trait behind it, but he had in Annalyla. An unsolicited opinion, something she'd come up with entirely on her own.

Acceptance.

More and more, the woman touched him in ways he could hardly comprehend.

For lack of a better response, he took her hand and lifted it to his lips, kissing it tenderly. Then, he smiled at her, watching her smile broaden in return. Perhaps he didn't need words, after all. Looking into her face, he could see that she understood without the benefit of an explanation.

She could see how much her acceptance of his oddity meant to him.

"Come," he said softly, pulling her to her feet and taking the empty cup from her hands, setting it aside. "Walk with me. See this empire we now rule over."

Annalyla went with him gladly. She was still in her heavy green cloak; she'd slept in the thing, so as they headed to the big entry, she brushed the dirt from the hall off of it. Once she stopped brushing and her head came up, she could see that the fog had lifted, but there were storm clouds overhead and a steady rain was falling.

Somewhere, thunder rolled in the distance. But for the most part, it was a peaceful rain. Pulling the hood of the cloak over her freshly-braided hair, Annalyla headed out into the bailey with Tenner, which she immediately noticed was cobbled. She hadn't noticed it last night, and it was a very strange thing to see a cobbled bailey, with hundreds of stones to make a hard surface of sorts. Her confusion must have registered on her face because Tenner seemed to read her thoughts.

"I, too, was surprised to see the cobbled bailey," he said, grinning at her when she looked up at him in surprise. "I have only seen a few of these, and usually at castles that suffer a great deal of rain. Putting stones down like this is meant to prevent the bailey from becoming pitted with holes and grooves as the dirt is washed away by the rain. I can only imagine that this was done to prevent such a thing, as I am sure there is a good deal of rainfall here and mist from the ocean. The sea salt eats away at everything."

Annalyla nodded in understanding as they picked their way over the wet stones. "It seems so odd that such care would be taken with the bailey of a derelict castle," she said. "I wonder who would take the time and expense to do this?"

Tenner glanced back at the big walls and the gatehouse, where his men were already working on figuring out the portcullis, which they had discovered to be jammed up into the second floor of the gatehouse.

"Whoever built the walls must have done this to the bailey," he said. "The Lords of Truro, I would think. They owned this property for many years and I would imagine that men were stationed here at one time."

"But something drove them away."

He looked at her curiously. "Why would you say that?"

She shrugged, looking at the ground as she walked so she wouldn't slip. "I heard the howling last night," she said. "Mayhap the rumors of the Devil of Baiadepaura are true. Mayhap, it was the ghost of the wicked lord that chased the men away."

He knew what she was talking about. Right after he'd left the hall last night, he'd been standing near the path that led down to the cove below when he'd heard a strange, haunting howl go hurling through the bailey. Every man in his command had heard it, and every man had been spooked by it. All night, they'd been waiting for more howling, or worse, the appearance of the creature making those terrible noises. Though nothing had appeared, this morning, he could still see the nervousness in their tired faces.

"It was the wind," he said simply. "No one saw a ghost."

He sounded sure of himself and Annalyla felt rather foolish for mentioning the ghost. What if he didn't believe in such things? He would think she was a silly fool.

"You… do not think it was the ghost we heard?"

"I do not think it was the ghost we heard," he said steadily. "Do you truly believe I would bring you to a place that was haunted by the specter of a murdered lord?"

Now she was feeling increasingly foolish. "Nay, Tenner."

She sounded contrite and he looked at her, feeling guilty that he'd sounded harsh with her. She didn't deserve that, so he lifted her hand and kissed it again.

"I did not mean to scold you," he said. "We are people of the civilized world and not barbarians who bay at the moon. I do not believe in ghosts; I believe everything has a logical explanation. Unless, and until, I see a ghost planted in front of me, I will continue to believe there are rational explanations for everything. And the stories that Graham told you were simply that – stories."

She forced a smile at him, nodding her head. "I will try not to be frightened of howling."

He chuckled. "If it is particularly menacing howling, I may very well be afraid, too."

He had the ability to soothe whatever foolishness she was feeling and her smile turned genuine. "I cannot believe you would be afraid of anything," she said. "You are a de Velt. A de Velt male knows no fear."

He lifted his dark eyebrows at her. "Who told you that? There is plenty I am fearful of."

"Like what?"

"You."

She looked at him in surprise. "Why on earth should I frighten you?"

He was playing it rather coy. "You are brave and beautiful and intelligent," he said. "That is a fearsome creature, indeed, something that makes men feel most unworthy."

She came to a halt, looking at him as the rain fell gently around them. "If anyone is unworthy, it is I," she said seriously. "You know that our betrothal was based on deception. You were gracious enough to forgive that deceit. Most men would not have. You are a most worthy man, Tenner, much more worthy than I could ever be."

He shook his head. "You have no idea how wrong that statement is," he said softly. "How fortunate I am that your father lied to my father, or I would not have had this chance at happiness. That is how I look at this, Annie – a chance I never thought I would have."

A smile spread across her lips. "You called me Annie."

"If it offends you, I will not do it again. I heard Maude call you the name and I like it."

Annalyla shook her head quickly, putting a hand on his big arm. "I am pleased that you are comfortable enough to call me that," she said. "I like it, too, when you say it."

With that, he took the drape of hair hanging over the right side of this face and tucked it back, behind his ear, revealing the eye with the green streak through it. She smiled broadly at the gesture, for it meant something to her. Now, it meant something to him.

Trust.

He grinned at her, struggling to get used to the fact that the eye was exposed. He wanted very much to let the hair fall over his face again, but he didn't. She liked him when his face and that eye were fully exposed.

He wanted to please her.

Taking her hand, he led her towards the keep, the shell of a building and only a hint of the former glory it once was. Once they passed inside, Annalyla removed her hood and began looking around with interest.

"As you can see, this is a big structure," Tenner said. "At least the keep has doors. We found them in another room, abandoned. I do not know who removed them, or why, but I have men who are skilled enough to rehang them."

Annalyla peered at the doorjamb, made of stone but overlaid with a wooden door frame; she could see it, weathered and worn. "Is this the only way in and out?"

He shook his head. "Nay," he said. "There is a servant's entrance on the north side where the kitchen is. There is a well and a kiln, and the cliff falls away slightly and there are stairs down into a kitchen which is remarkably intact. There is a vault attached to the kitchen, most of which runs beneath the north wing and beneath the central building we are standing in. I have not yet looked at the content of the vault, except to inspect it for any living creatures, but when we were down there last night, there seemed to be a good deal of clutter."

"I will go through it," Annalyla volunteered quickly. "The keep is my domain, is it not? I think Maude and I should go through it and see if there is anything salvageable. You have more important things to do than worry about an old storage vault."

"Are you sure? It will be dirty work."

"I am sure," she said confidently. "Do you suppose the previous lords left anything behind?"

"If they did, it should be quite old and ruined by now."

"Whatever I find, if it is anything of value, they cannot have it back."

He laughed at her, softly. She seemed determined and he did not argue with her or try to change her mind about digging around in the cold, dark vault. He simply smiled at her, as if he approved of her industrious statement, before looking around the stone walls, feeling the cold sea breeze blowing in through the windows that faced west.

"I am hoping to at least have the portcullises in place by tonight to protect us, as well as anything of value you might find," he said. "The men are working on the main gatehouse as we speak. In fact, the portcullis is there. We simply couldn't see it last night. It is wedged up into the second floor of the gatehouse and the men are trying to determine how to lower it. The gatehouse to the south, the small one, also has a portcullis that we found propped up against the southern wall."

"That seems strange," Annalyla said. "I wonder who would do that."

Tenner shook his head. "I do not know, but we will restore it," he said confidently. "Now, the keep, for the most part, seems intact except for the second floor of the northern wing. Part of the wall has crumbled and the roof is missing. For now, we can simply shut off that chamber until it can be repaired, but the rest of the keep is livable. It needs a good sweeping, but it is livable. The ground level has seven chambers, including what looks to be a rather large solar, and then the upper floor, excluding the two damaged chambers in the northern wing, has two big chambers above us and another two big chambers in the southern wing. I will show them to you. You can choose the ones you wish. I shall give

Maude and Arlo the others."

Annalyla was eager to see the chambers and Tenner took her up a flight of rather slippery stone steps to the chamber above. As he'd told her, they were livable, with a surprisingly solid roof, but there was a good deal of dust and bird droppings. Sea birds had made their nests in the some of the ceiling joists. She peered at the nests, which were now empty, before moving into the two chambers in the southern wing. As soon as she walked into the larger of the chambers and saw the view, she gasped softly.

"*This* chamber," she said, her gaze on the grayish-green sea beyond. "What a beautiful view of the sea we shall have."

Tenner walked up behind her, looking over her shoulder as the rain fell upon the sea. "Then we shall have this chamber and the adjoining one for our personal use," he said. "If you and Maude would like to start sweeping out the keep, I can have the quartermaster bring in the bedding. With everything so wet, however, I am not entirely sure what we will stuff the mattress with at this point."

She turned to look at him. "Is there a bed frame?"

He nodded. "Knowing that there would be women with us, I brought two beds from Seven Crosses," he said. "We shall have a bed frame and a table, and a few other things to make this place more comfortable."

Annalyla was relieved to hear that. A little comfort was a good thing. "We can also use a few servants," she said. "Mayhap, you can find some in the town to the north, the one we passed by on our way here. A few female servants to help us clean this place, and a kitchen servant or two would be good. And a cook – unless you want me cooking your meals for the rest of my life, we could use a cook, as well."

He laughed softly. "You do not wish to cook for me for the rest of your life? I am crushed."

She laughed in return. "Last night's meal was a miracle, believe me," she said. "It was pure luck that everything turned out as it should. I should not like to test that luck indefinitely. You may end up sending me back to Roseden to save your stomach."

"Never," he said firmly. "You will never be out of my sight, ever. You belong to me now and I intend to keep you, bad cooking or no."

Annalyla couldn't help but smile at the man. It seemed as if all she did was smile at him, for there was so very much to smile about. A marriage that agreed with her, a husband she was coming to adore... her life at Roseden, and the crushing presence of Mother Angel and her father, seemed years ago. She almost couldn't remember them. In a bold move, she went to Tenner and put her arms around his waist, showing him the affection she was coming to feel for the man. It was difficult not to show it.

"Thank you for keeping me," she said, feeling the thrill of his embrace as he wrapped his arms around her. "And thank you for trusting me with my duties. I was thinking... this may be a derelict old castle but, to me, it is the most beautiful castle in the world because it belongs to us. Mayhap that sounds silly, but it is the way I feel."

Tenner held her snuggly against him, looking down into those wide, green eyes that were so bright with life and beauty.

"It is the way I feel also," he admitted. "You said that with a de Velt in command, perfection is assured. You could not know how badly I needed to hear those words, Annie. I do not know what I was expecting, but when we arrived yesterday, a broken-down castle was not among those expectations. Thank you for keeping my spirits up."

She was sweetly flattered by his words. "I will always keep your spirits up," she said. "And I shall always tell you the truth. The truth, at the moment, is that you are exhausted and I must clean this chamber so that the bed may be brought in. When it is, you should try to sleep, at least for a few hours. Will you do this for me?"

He thought to dispute her but realized he could not. All of his men needed to sleep, and a rainy afternoon was perhaps the best time to do it. In surrender, he nodded.

"I will," he said. "But what are you going to stuff the mattress with? Everything is wet."

Annalyla turned to the window facing over the sea. Down below were a small clearing and the sea path that Tenner's men were beginning to destroy. But surrounding the cliffs and castle were growths of scrub grass and bushes that looked springy and full. Because of the rain, everything was lush and green for the most part. She pointed out of the window.

"See all of that scrub foliage that your men are carving up?" she said as he came to the window. "Bring as much of it as you can to the great hall and we'll dry it out in the warmth of the hall. We can stuff the mattresses with that. At the moment, I do not see any alterative."

Tenner didn't either. He put his big arm around her shoulders. "You are clever as well as industrious," he said. "I will have the men start bringing it in now. As for servants, Ivor has small outposts in Bude and Widemouth, but I do not think I can pick them clean for their servants. They are very small posts. That being the case, I shall send Graham into town to procure a few. We may have to pay them quite well considering their place of employment will be Baiadepaura, but I am willing to do so. This is a big place and you cannot do all of the work yourself."

"Thank you, my lord."

With a plan of action set for the day, there was no time to waste. Taking Annalyla's hand, Tenner led her back down the stairs and out of the cold, drafty keep, returning her to the hall where he explained their plans for the day to Maude, Arlo, and Graham, who had gathered near the fire after a long and damp night.

As Graham dutifully headed off to the nearby village to the north in search of servants, Arlo and Tenner headed outside where the soldiers were destroying the path from the sea. Once Tenner arrived, some of the men were taken off of the path duty and put to work cutting up the heavy scrub that was growing wild all along the cliff's edge.

When the scrub began to come into the hall in loads, Annalyla and Maude had built up the fire in the pit so much that the hall was quite warm, and they beat at the shrubs in order to shake off the water so they would start to dry out. But the looming issue of cleaning up their sleeping chambers in the keep was hanging over their heads, so the women left some soldiers in charge of drying out the sea scrub while they collected buckets of water, lye soap, and brooms that the quartermaster had brought along, and headed into the keep to clean.

In truth, Annalyla had never felt more useful or more industrious. It was a joyful chore that she undertook with gusto. And as the rain began to lighten and the sun began peeking out of the clouds, Annalyla swept floors and scrubbed down walls, trying to make the old keep livable.

Trying to make the old bones of Baiadepaura Castle a home.

But the worst was yet to come.

CHAPTER ELEVEN

HER NAME WAS Mawgwen.

She was a very old woman with an old crow perched on her shoulder, and she came into the bailey of Baiadepaura with five other timid women. They were followed by Graham, who was literally herding the small group and had all the way from the town.

It was nearing the nooning meal and it hadn't taken Graham but a few hours to locate enough women willing to take quite a bit of money to serve at Baiadepaura under Tenner de Velt and the Earl of Tiverton. Graham was able to convince the women that the coin was worth the risk, and that there were so many soldiers at Baiadepaura that any ghost would be foolish to show himself. But the boast about the soldiers didn't do any more for Graham's cause than the lure of money did.

It was the only reason the women had come.

Jobs were scarce along this stretch of the Cornwall coast, so it was pure economics that forced six women from the Bude to accept the offer of employment at Baiadepaura, and their need for coin overcame their fear of the castle, at least for the moment. But all of them had lived in Bude their entire lives, and they knew well the stories of the haunted castle on the cliff's edge.

Annalyla could see that fear in their eyes as they entered the bailey carrying their worldly possessions with them. The bailey was being cleaned by a small army of soldiers, using shovels and picks to rid the bailey the piles of earth and fill the holes in the cobbling that had occurred from sheer neglect.

As the group worked on the bailey, the portcullises, both of them, had been returned to their original positions. The one in the south gatehouse was being secured into a permanent position, one that could not be opened and merely acted as part of the wall, while the one in the main gatehouse was being furiously worked on by another army of soldiers because Tenner wanted the portcullis secured by nightfall. He didn't want to spend another night in a castle that he was unable to fortify.

It was into this chaos that Mawgwen and the other women came, and Annalyla and Maude were there to greet them beneath a sky that was remarkably clear considering how bad the weather had been as of late. The sun was drying out the mud and warming the land, and the day was actually quite pleasant. But it wasn't enough to make Baiadepaura look inviting; Annalyla knew that. She knew that was why she saw such apprehension on the faces of the women who had come to serve.

"I am Lady de Velt," she said to the group as Graham brought them near. "My husband is the commander of Baiadepaura Castle, and you shall take your orders from me and from Lady de Correa."

She was indicating Maude, who had more experience handling servants than Annalyla had. In fact, Maude stepped forward, seeing the fearful faces, and spoke firmly.

"You have come to work at a good wage," she said sternly. "We have no time for foolery. If you do not think you can accomplish your tasks, then tell me now. I do not want to have to tell you twice for things that must be done. If I must do that, then I shall dismiss you without any pay at all. Is that understood?"

The women nodded uneasily, looking at each other, looking to the castle beyond as if they were about to enter the gates of Hell itself. Maude saw that anxiety but she ignored it. The best thing to do was to get the women working right away, and she intended to do just that.

"Now," she said. "I need at least two kitchen servants. Who has had experience in the kitchen?"

That was when Mawgwen lifted her hand, upsetting her crow. The bird screeched unhappily.

"I have, milady," she said with a heavy Cornish accent. "These other ladies have served in taverns and inns. One served the local church by cleaning up after the priests. We'll not disappoint ye, milady, but ye must know that Baiadepaura has cast fear into their hearts."

Maude looked at the old woman; she was short and round, with wild gray hair escaping from a brown cap that the crow was picking at. She lifted a disapproving eyebrow.

"What is your name?" she asked.

"Mawgwen, milady."

"We do not want that bird around the food. If it is a pet, I shall not deny you, but it cannot be in the kitchen."

The old woman looked at the bird. "Does ye hear that?" she asked. "Ye must behave yerself or end up in a pie."

The bird flapped its wings and dumped white bird feces right onto the woman's shoulder, which Mawgwen ignored as if it weren't any concern at all. Maude's face twisted with disgust as Annalyla took over for fear that Maude was about to scold the woman and send her away. As far as Annalyla was concerned, they needed *all* of the women. A morning of cleaning and scrubbing had left her with red hands, an aching back, and the realization that they badly needed help.

"The bird can remain, but please make sure he is not around the food," she said. "Mawgwen, you may come with me. I am overseeing the kitchens while Lady de Correa is overseeing the final touches on the keep and then the hall." She turned to Maude. "I will take two of them with me and you take the rest. Make sure the quartermaster brings all of his supplies down to the kitchen so that we can organize everything for the evening meal."

Maude nodded, pulling out four women and taking them with her towards the keep. That left Annalyla with Mawgwen and a tiny, skinny, redheaded girl named Mercy. She indicated for the women to follow her as they headed off to the north side of the keep where the stairs led down to the kitchens.

"We heard tale of an army at Baiadepaura, milady," Mawgwen said as she shuffled after her. "Ye came yesterday, did ye?"

Annalyla nodded. "We did," she said. "We did not expect to find the place in such terrible repair. It will take a lot of work to make it livable again."

Mawgwen was slightly behind her. The crow screeched again as the old woman shifted the bundle she was carrying, a worn satchel and then more possessions that were all wrapped up in a shawl.

"Did ye find anyone here when ye came, milady?" she asked.

"We did not."

"Then ye don't know that the pirates have been using Baiadepaura."

Annalyla came to a halt and looked at her. "Pirates?" she repeated. "What pirates?"

Mawgwen shifted her burden again and the crow, incensed with all of the jostling, took off and flew to the roofline of the castle, screeching loudly. But the old woman ignored the bird.

"Why, the men who sail the *Beast of the Seas*," she said. "Everyone knows of it. They sail up and down the coast, and they have been using Baiadepaura Castle for quite some time. They live here and keep their ship docked in the cove below. Does yer husband not know this?"

Annalyla didn't know if he did or not, but she didn't want to make Tenner look stupid. "I am sure he knows everything," she said confidently, but she wasn't, not really. "But… but the pirates are not here now. They are not coming back."

Mawgwen lifted her eyebrows in a gesture that suggested disbelief, but she didn't say so. She pretended to believe the young woman's words. "That is good," she said. "Ye don't need pirates when ye already have enough to worry about with the place."

"What do you mean?"

"Why, the curse, of course," she said. "Don't tell me that ye don't know of the curse, milady. Everyone in England knows that Baiadepaura Castle is haunted with the ghost of an evil lord."

There was talk of the curse again, now from a local. It was one thing to hear it from Graham, who knew it as a child. But it was another thing to hear it from someone who lived near the castle. Perhaps, the old woman knew much more than Graham or even Tenner knew. Although Annalyla knew she shouldn't ask, something in her just couldn't help it.

"I have heard some stories," she admitted. "But tell me what *you* know of it. And do not leave anything out."

The old woman's eyes glittered. When speaking of the legend of Baiadepaura, there was no need to embellish.

The truth was bad enough.

"Come, Lady de Velt," she said, nodding her head in the direction of the kitchens. "Let us find the kitchen and begin our tasks, and I'll tell ye want ye want to know."

Annalyla thought there was a hint of foreboding in that statement.

Try as she might, she couldn't seem to shake it.

THE CROW STOOD in the doorway to the kitchen, pacing and chattering. He never tried to enter the chamber, which was all well and good, but he certainly made his displeasure known at being kept outside. As the young girl, Mercy, began to clean up one section of the derelict old kitchen, Mawgwen and Annalyla inspected the hearth that was large enough to roast an entire cow.

"It has been a long time since I've seen this kitchen," Mawgwen said, peering up the chimney. "I was but a young *mos* when I came here with my grandmother, who served the Lords of Truro. That was many years ago, milady."

Annalyla looked at her. "*Mos*," she repeated. "What does that mean?"

Mawgwen smiled, showing what teeth she had left. "It means girl in the Cornish," she said. "Cornish is a language all its own. It is a special language, one of pride. We still speak it in Cornwall."

Annalyla found that rather interesting. "I did not realize that," she said. "Mayhap, you can teach it to me. I should like to learn it if my husband is to be stationed here. It would be good to know."

Mawgwen nodded. "I should like to, milady," she said. Her gaze lingered on Annalyla for a moment. "But ye don't want to talk of the Cornish, do ye? Ye want to know of Baiadepaura."

Annalyla did, but she eyed the old lady with some suspicion. "I do," she said. "But I want to know something first."

"What is it, milady?"

"If this place is so haunted, why did you come?"

"Because ye need to know about Baiadepaura, milady," she said. "When we heard there was an army come, I knew ye didn't know everything. That's why I come."

"To warn us?"

"To tell ye what ye're facing."

Annalyla folded her arms over her chest, trying to project a strong front but perhaps looking just the least bit fearful instead.

"Go ahead, then," she said. "Tell me about this place."

Mawgwen did. "My family has lived in the village for centuries, milady," she said. "There is a story my grandmother told me, that her grandmother told her. Many years ago, after the Romans left these shores and the age of darkness descended on the land, there was a wicked lord who ruled over Baiadepaura. He brought a great sickness to the land, cursing the villagers, and they rebelled against him. It is that lord whose ghost wanders the grounds."

In spite of her determination not to be spooked, Annalyla couldn't help the return of her sense of doom, the same sense of doom she'd had when they'd first arrived. A wicked lord and ghostly wanderings… she could feel the hair standing up on the back of her neck.

"What is his name?" she asked.

"Faustus," Mawgwen said. "Faustus de Paura. The castle is named for the bay, and the bay is named for his family – de Paura."

Annalyla had already heard that from Graham, but she wanted to know if the old woman knew anything different. Given that it was the same thing, it confirmed what Graham had told her. It also made her wonder if everything Graham told her was truth and not simply local legend, which was an unsettling thought.

"But why does he wander?" she asked. "What does he want?"

Mawgwen held up a finger. "Ah," she said. "'Tis not what he wants. 'Tis what he's looking for."

"What is he looking for?"

Mawgwen turned and waddled over to her belongings, which she'd placed against the wall when they'd entered the kitchen.

"Many years ago, my grandfather's grandfather was part of the group of villagers that came to Baiadepaura to rid the land of the wicked lord once and for all," she said. "He came with many other villagers, hoping that by killing the wicked lord, it would destroy the curse that had consumed the land. But their hope was in vain; they killed the man and his wicked wife, and the curse continued. Now, it hovers over Baiadepaura like a shadow, waiting to be called forth again."

Annalyla watched the woman as she dug around in her satchel before finally pulling forth something that was wrapped up in a length of dirty canvas that smelled of earth. As she turned back to Annalyla, she continued speaking, her voice now considerably softer.

"My grandfather's grandfather took this from Baiadepaura on the night the wicked lord was killed," she said, unwrapping the canvas. "I am going to give it to ye, milady. It is the curse, written by the wicked lord himself. When ye leave this place, ye must leave this curse behind, within these old walls. If ye do not, then the curse will follow ye wherever ye go."

With that, the canvas wrapping fell away and she extended what looked to be a piece of rolled hide, old and brittle and yellowed.

Annalyla looked at it for several long moments without accepting it.

"Why should you give me the written curse?" she asked. "I have nothing to do with it."

A dark gleam came to the old woman's eyes. "Ye had everything to do with it when yer husband assumed command of Baiadepaura," she said in a tone that sounded like a growl. "Take it; it is part of ye now. But ye must leave it behind when ye go, and the sooner the better. Don't let this curse have time to sink its claws into ye. The longer ye stay, the worse it will be."

Annalyla received the clear impression that Mawgwen was advising her to leave immediately, but she knew Tenner never would. It was a foolish suggestion, really. They'd only just arrived. With a sharp sigh, she reached out and took the hide, but she didn't unroll it. She simply held it.

"You did not answer my question," she said. "What is the ghost looking for?"

Mawgwen could see that her warning was having no effect. "My grandfather told me that when the lord's wife was killed, an amulet in the shape of a horsehead was taken from her," the old woman said, displeased that her admonition had gone unheeded. "His grandfather told him that someone stole it from her body, but the man who stole it was killed even before he left Baiadepaura. Somehow, the fire that had engulfed the lord and his wife also engulfed him, and there were whispers that he was cursed for stealing the amulet. Therefore, it is not known if the amulet made it out of Baiadepaura and the ghost has been looking for it ever since."

"But why?"

"Who's to say? It belonged to his wife and he wants it back."

A ghost, a curse, and now a missing amulet. Annalyla was increasingly spooked, but far more interested in the history of Baiadepaura, and the story of the curse, than she cared to admit. It was fascinating and frightening at the same time. She knew the old woman was trying to warn her off, but it was advice that would go ignored. She and

Tenner were here, and they were here to stay. Her gaze moved to the old hide in her hands.

"Have you read the curse?" she asked.

Mawgwen shook her head. "Nay, milady," she said. "It is not my right. The curse does not belong to me. Now, it belongs to ye. Ye must read it and ye must leave tonight, or the Devil of Baiadepaura will come for ye."

Now, the old woman's warnings were sounding like a threat. Annalyla didn't like the fact that the woman was trying to force her, and everyone else, out of Baiadepaura with tales of this alleged curse. Perhaps it was only a warning of concern, but something didn't seem right to Annalyla.

Something was off.

It was quite a neat little story, and almost *too* convenient. Annalyla wasn't the suspicious type, but something about old Mawgwen didn't seem right. She knew everything about the castle and the curse, and she was pushing hard to get them out of there. In fact, Annalyla wasn't entirely sure she wanted the woman cooking their food. If she wanted them out badly enough, she might try to poison them.

But Annalyla didn't let on her suspicions. For now, Mawgwen was a source of information about the castle and she wasn't ready to let that go just yet. She had the old hide and she wanted to show it to Tenner to see what he thought about all of this.

"I thank you for your concern, Mawgwen," she said politely. "I shall give this to my husband. Meanwhile, please see about cleaning out the hearth and I shall return as soon as I can."

Mawgwen nodded, watching the young woman leave with the rolled hide in her hand. She could only imagine what the woman's husband would say now that his wife held the very curse that the legend sprang from. It was, in fact, the actual hide Mawgwen's great-great-grandfather had taken from Baiadepaura the night the wicked lord was killed. At least, that's what she'd been told, and it had been passed down in her family for generations.

It was simply a convenient fact that it was in her possession.

But now that she'd passed it to the young lady, surely her husband would take his army and flee for fear of rousing the Devil of Baiadepaura. Surely, they would leave by nightfall.

At least, that was the hope.

Mawgwen didn't see much use in cleaning the hearth now, but she went about it, anyway. She'd done what had been asked of her by the big, redheaded Scots pirate who had shown up at her door before dawn. He knew her, and had for years, and he knew about the rolled hide that was in her family's possession. Nearly everyone in Bude knew it, too, so it wasn't a secret. Mawgwen Coombe's family had been in the area for centuries, and everyone knew of their link to Baiadepaura. The pirate had given her a sack full of gold coins in exchange for that rolled hide and a little visit to the castle her ancestor had once sacked.

Now, all there was to do was wait.

The curse, or the fear of it, would take care of the rest.

CHAPTER TWELVE

CONTRARY TO WHAT Annalyla had told Mawgwen, she didn't seek Tenner.

Quite honestly, she wasn't sure she would. Her reasonable, stalwart husband didn't believe in curses or ghosts; he'd made that clear. Therefore, she didn't want to look like a silly fool by bringing in an old curse written on a sheep's hide if, in fact, it was even a curse.

She wanted to check it out for herself.

Heading out of the kitchen and into the afternoon, which was turning cool as clouds once again began to gather and a stiff breeze came from the sea, Annalyla could already see men with foodstuffs for the kitchen departing the hall and heading in her direction. She paused a moment, pointing to the kitchen stairs and telling them to deliver their goods down into the kitchen and attached vault, which reminded her that she needed to check the vault sooner rather than later.

She had many duties to complete and little time to do them in, but she was happy to be busy. More men moved past her, swiftly, and she could see Graham also heading in her direction. The older knight looked weary, his weathered face lined with exhaustion.

"You should rest, Graham," she said as he came near. "You look very tired."

The man nodded, running his fingers through his graying hair. "I am," he said. "So many years at Roseden with very little to do, and suddenly I am back in action, as I was when I was a young knight. It is rather exciting, I must say."

Annalyla grinned at his enthusiasm. "Even so, you should rest," she said. "Tenner is in our chamber even now, sleeping. The mattresses were stuffed a little while ago and when I left him, he was crawling into bed. There are several chambers on the floor of the keep. You may take one for your private use if you wish. There is one near the entry that may be quite suitable for you."

Graham looked in the direction of the keep. "Indeed," he said, finally letting his guard down. Exhaustion was in everything about him. "I shall do as you suggest."

"Good," Annalyla said. "And – Graham?"

"Aye?"

"Those women you brought… where did you find them?"

He threw a thumb in a generally northward direction. "There is a tavern at the southern edge of Bude," he said. "They were all there. In fact, it was rather odd… as if they were just waiting for me to come in there and offer them jobs."

Annalyla cocked her head. "That does seem strange," she said. "Did they say they were waiting for a job – *any* job?"

He nodded. "The innkeeper told me that people often gather there in the hope that merchants or ships will need workers, so it is evidently not unusual for the desperate and unemployed to gather there," he said. "Still, when I entered and mentioned where I was from, they all seemed very eager to go with me."

"Even the old woman? Mawgwen?"

"Especially her," Graham said. "She told me that it was fortuitous that I had come to the tavern because she was preparing to come to Baiadepaura and offer her services. She was the most eager of all to come. Why? Did she say something to you?"

Annalyla eyed him. She didn't want to tell him what the woman had really said, at least not all of it. She was afraid Graham would go off on more tales of curses about Baiadepaura and how he had been right all along. She didn't think Tenner would like it if he caught wind of such a thing, because he'd been annoyed from the outset that Graham had told her stories about Baiadepaura. Therefore, she kept silent on the matter.

"Not really," she said after a moment. "But she does know a great deal about Baiadepaura. She said her grandfather's grandfather was part of the mob that killed the wicked lord of Baiadepaura."

"Is that so?" Graham looked interested, but only momentarily. "Then, mayhap, that was why she was so eager to come – to return to the scene of her ancestor's crime."

Annalyla snorted. "Mayhap that is true, but I think she will be a wealth of information on the history of the castle. What we know seems to be legends and rumors, nothing of fact. She may know fact."

"Or she may make things worse."

"Time will tell, I suppose."

Graham scratched his head again. His interest in old Mawgwen was finished as thoughts of sleep filled his mind. He pointed to the keep.

"A chamber near the entry, you say?"

Annalyla nodded. "To the left," she said, pointing. "It is yours, Graham. But be mindful – Tenner is sleeping upstairs. The last I saw, men were trying to hang the doors to the keep, so tell them to be quiet."

Graham waved her off, heading towards the keep. Annalyla watched him go for a few moments before returning her attention to the brittle hide in her hand. She very much wanted to unroll it and see what was really written on it, if anything at all, but she didn't want to do it out here for all to see. She wanted to look at it privately, like a wicked little secret she wanted to keep concealed for the moment. Therefore, she followed Graham's path to the keep because that was a place where she could find some privacy.

She knew just the room.

Tenner had already laid claim to the large chamber overlooking the bailey, with the view of the gatehouse and hall and nearly everything else. It had four big lancet windows that assured an excellent view of most of the complex, and Annalyla knew that Tenner wanted this chamber as his solar, a place for him to conduct his business as garrison commander.

It was a chamber to the right off the entry and across from the room she'd suggested for Graham. It had big double-doors that were surprisingly intact even if they were a bit warped. Heading into the cold, dark chamber, she closed the doors for some privacy before moving to the windows where there was still a good amount of light filtering in.

For a moment, she simply inspected the hide. It was cracked and fragile, and she carefully unrolled it, wondering what she was about to see. It could be nothing, or it could be everything Mawgwen said it was. It could be a fraud, but there was no way to know that. It certainly looked old enough that it could have been written two centuries earlier, but she truly had no idea if it was or not. She unrolled it completely and turned it around to the bare surface, seeing the faint etchings on the hide that were stained deep into the flesh.

There was something there.

Curiosity overtook Annalyla as she held the hide up to the light see what, exactly, had been written. The ink was faded, and brown, but it had stained the hide long ago, so much so that even the passing of the years couldn't erase it. The print was legible and she could immediately see that the words were Latin. Having been educated in a fine house, Annalyla had been taught to both read and write Latin because it was the language of the church. In order to read one's prayer book, one had to know how to read it. Most noble women knew Latin. Peering closely at the words, she began to read.

Quidam amici – doleo propter passionem consummare. Ego quoque sum patiens. Hoc est quod fecit te fecit etiam valetudine mea. Permitto tibi. Mea uxor, mea Anyu, quia bene pati. Nos innocentes. Ego oro ad finem doloris tui. Si potui loqui, ut non dicam tibi quod sit in corde et lingua mea capta est natus.

Nolite quaeso odio. Placere parcere. Obsecro per misericordiam, et miserationes. Ego autem non haec languorem vobis.

Annalyla's breath caught in her throat.

She read it three times in full, and then skimmed through it, picking out certain phrases. The truth was that the missive could have been written by anyone, and it could have addressed a dozen different situations with the message the words conveyed. But the signature at the bottom told her that, indeed, she had something authentic on her hands. The name signed at the bottom of the document said it all – *di Paura.*

But it was more than that.

The message didn't contain a curse. She'd been clearly led to believe that it had, but it didn't. In truth, what she was reading was horrific at best, considering what she'd been told about the legend of Baiadepaura – that a wicked lord and his wife had been killed for their evil deeds, and old Mawgwen had sworn that what was written upon this hide was a curse written by the lord himself. Something wicked, spit out of the fire-tipped fingers of a wicked man.

But what Annalyla read was anything but wicked.

Confusion swept her. Taking a deep breath, she read aloud in hushed tones.

"Kind friends – I am sorry for your suffering. I, too, am suffering. That which has caused your illness has also caused mine. I suffer with you. My wife, my dear Anyu, suffers as well. But we are innocent. I will pray for your suffering to end. If I could speak, I could tell you what is in my heart, but God has taken my voice.

Please do not hate. Please show mercy. I beg for pity and compassion. I did not bring this sickness upon you."

Shocked, she simply stared at the words. It sounded like pleading. *Begging.* The man who wrote it was asking for pity and compassion. He wasn't slinging curses and hatred.

Nay, this didn't make any sense at all.

"Di Paura," she whispered. "God's Bones… why did you write such a message? Is all not what it seems?"

There was no reply to her softly-uttered question. She hadn't expected one. But the more she looked at the writing, the more it began to occur to her that, indeed, perhaps not all was at it seemed. Perhaps the legend was about someone else for, certainly, it could not be about the man who had written these sorrowful words.

It was a mistake.

Perhaps the entire legend was a mistake.

"*But God has taken my tongue*," she murmured to herself, reading over those words. She thought hard on them. "The man could not speak? Surely… surely this cannot be the lord who roams these halls. It must be someone else. Clearly, this man is pleading for his life."

Only the wind answered. At least, she thought it was the wind. Something brushed up against her and when she glanced up, all she could see was a mist. It was like the fog that so often settled on these cliffs, but at the moment, there was no fog. The sun was still shining even though clouds were gathering.

The air was clear.

But there was a fog inside the chamber. Baffled, Annalyla watched as the mist seemed to take a shape. It all happened rather quickly, so there was no real time to react. But the mist undulated into the shape of a man and a ghostly hand reached out, brushing against her. The moment it touched her, it felt as if great shards of ice raced through her body. Everything turned cold.

"*Anyu equi.*"

Annalyla heard the words, but they weren't spoken. It was as if someone had exhaled in her ear; the words were mouthed upon a breath, a hiss of something unseen and unknown.

Anyu equi.

Before Annalyla could show any fear at all, the misty man disappeared, fading away as if he'd never been. Once there, he was now swiftly gone, causing Annalyla to question what she had really seen.

"Annie?"

A shout on the other side of the door nearly scared Annalyla right out of her skin and she shrieked in fear, unable to stop herself. The door suddenly flew open and Maude was standing there, looking at her with a mixture of concern and fright.

"Annie!" she gasped. "What's wrong?"

Annalyla was nearly stiff with terror. Her mouth was hanging open and it took her a moment to reclaim her wits as she realized she'd just seen a ghost. *A ghost who put words in her ear!*

She waved her hand frantically at Maude.

"Close the door!" she hissed. "Close it, I say!"

Confused at the sense of urgency in Annalyla's manner, Maude did as she was told. She closed the warped door and turned to Annalyla, greatly concerned.

"Why?" she demanded softly. "Annie, what's wrong?"

Annalyla's eyes were wide as she looked at Maude. She hardly knew where to start. "I…" she stammered. Then, she swallowed and started again. "Oh, Maude… you must look at this. It is written in Latin, but you must… you *must* read it."

Maude was puzzled. She went to Annalyla, looking at the hide in her hands and the faded writing upon the brittle yellow skin.

"What is it?" she asked.

Annalyla realized that she was shaking. "The old woman, Mawgwen, gave it to me," she said. "She told me that the curse of Baiadepaura is written on this hide and that, now, the curse belongs to me."

Maude looked stricken. "A curse!"

But Annalyla shook her head quickly. "It is *not*," she insisted, extending the hide to her. "Maude, she told me it was a curse, but it is not.

I do not think she ever read it, 'else she would not have told me wrongly. I swear that it is not a curse. You must read it for yourself."

Maude eyed her; the woman wasn't making a lot of sense, but she dutifully read the missive in the faded brown ink, reading it carefully not once, but twice. By the third pass, her eyes were wide with astonishment.

"*Who* wrote this, Annie?" she asked.

Annalyla's gaze trailed to the signature at the bottom of the message. "It is signed *di Paura*," she said. "The castle is named for the family."

Maude was becoming increasingly astonished. "This is a… a *plea*. The man who wrote this is begging for mercy."

Annalyla nodded, her hands at her mouth as she tried to regain her composure. "I know," she murmured. "Mawgwen told me it was written by the wicked lord of Baiadepaura and that it was a curse. She said the very ghost that haunts these grounds is of the man who wrote it. But you have read what it says… clearly, it is not a curse. It is a missive written by a man pleading for compassion and understanding."

Maude nodded, looking back to the faded writing and read a passage that stood out to her. "*If I could speak, I could tell you what is in my heart, but God has taken my tongue.*" She looked at Annalyla again. "What do you suppose he means?"

Annalyla shook her head. "Mayhap… mayhap he was born without the ability to speak," she said. "Mayhap he was born without a tongue. Think on it, Maude; he could not speak, so when the villagers came, he could not tell them the truth. He could not tell them anything at all."

Maude pondered her reasoning, looking to the hide once more. It was as if she couldn't look away from it at all. "But he *could* write," she said. "That means he had some education, even if he could not speak."

Annalyla looked at her as if something great had just occurred to her. "Graham told me that the last lord of Baiadepaura was responsible for a plague that swept the area," she said, pointing to the writing. "Wouldn't you say that this message alludes to that? He says he is sick and so is his wife, Anyu, but he also says he did not bring the sickness. That would confirm that at least part of the legend was true – that there *was* a sickness."

Maude nodded firmly. "It must have been something terrible," she agreed. "He asks for compassion and mercy. Annie… if this is the same ghost everyone speaks of, the one roaming the halls, what if he does not roam because of a curse. What… what if he roams for vengeance? Because he was wrongly killed?"

A great burst of wind suddenly hurled through the chamber, from one end to the other, causing both women to shriek in both fear and surprise. Annalyla and Maude latched on to one another, terrified as an icy wind enveloped them. In fact, the wind caught the hide in Maude's hand, tugging at it and, frightened, she let it go. It fell to the floor, kicked around by the wind, but as the wind escaped through the lancet windows, both women clearly heard a breathy whisper…

Anyu equi.

As quickly as the wind came, it was gone. The women looked at each other in fear before Annalyla released Maude and bent down to pick up the hide. Her hands were shaking worse than before.

"That happened before you came in," she said, her voice quivering. "You heard me cry out; it was because something touched me and I heard those same words – *Anyu equi.* Maude, the ghost knows we are here. He knows we have read his missive!"

Maude was pale with fright. "Will he turn his vengeance against us, I wonder?"

Annalyla took a deep breath, trying to steady herself. "I do not know," she said. "I hope not. Mawgwen told me that the ghost is looking for his wife's lost amulet, which was stolen from her when she was killed. The man who stole it was killed, also, so it is believed that the amulet itself is cursed. Mayhap, that is the true curse of Baiadepaura – the amulet itself. And mayhap, the ghost is not here to seek vengeance as much as he is here to reclaim the amulet that belonged to his wife."

Maude wasn't so sure. "How could you know that?"

Annalyla shook her head. "I do not," she said. "But what we heard – *Anyu equi* – means Anyu's horse. Even old Mawgwen said that the amulet is that of a horsehead. I have heard that the ghost is out to wreak havoc, or to curse anyone who sets foot in Baiadepaura, but Mawgwen told me he is looking for his wife's amulet – and somehow, I cannot believe a man who would write such a sorrowful missive to be so full of hate that he is looking to wreak havoc upon anyone who comes to his castle. Mayhap, he is simply here because he wants to find what had belonged to his wife. It must mean a great deal to him."

The more Maude thought about it, the more it made sense. "So how do we find it?" she asked. "It has been nearly two centuries, from what I've been told. The amulet is probably long gone. I would not even know where to start."

That was very true. Annalyla was feeling some defeat even as she nodded her head. "Mayhap," she said softly. "But I know someone to ask."

Maude knew exactly who she meant. "Let's find the old woman and see what she has to say about this," she said. "Do we tell her of the contents of the hide?"

Annalyla shook her head. "Nay," she said. "She thinks it is a curse. Let her think that for now. Maude, she was trying very hard to convince me to tell Tenner to leave this place. She wants us out; that is clear. I cannot imagine why she should be so concerned for our safety, so I must think that she has other reasons for wanting us out. I do not trust her. Therefore, tell her not what the missive truly says, but ask about that amulet. Mayhap, that is the key to all of this."

Maude nodded firmly. "Agreed."

Together, and with the hide in hand, the women left the solar with its warped doors and headed back to the kitchens.

They had an old woman to interrogate.

CHAPTER THIRTEEN

Already, there was a fire in the hearth of the kitchen at Baiadepaura, which wasn't such a good idea considering the chimney hadn't been used in years. Some smoke was escaping through the chimney, but it was also billowing out into the kitchen and lingering up near the ceiling. As Annalyla and Maude entered the kitchen, with the hide tucked up under Maude's arm, they couldn't help but cough at all of the smoke. The air in the chamber was positively blue because of it.

Mawgwen and Mercy were at the hearth, trying to unplug whatever might be jammed up into the chimney. Considering the fire in the hearth was fairly large, they were trying not to get burned. Mercy was ramming the handle of a broom up into the chimney and chunks of soot and dirt were falling out, but the old woman was calling her off, telling her that they'd done all they could. The young girl was setting the broom aside and returning to her chores just as the two ladies walked in.

"Mawgwen?" Annalyla said politely. "We have a need to speak with you."

The old woman was still looking up the chimney. "I know it," she said. "And I'm sorry for it. But I thought it best to start the fire now to see if the chimney needs unblocking. I know ye didn't tell me to, but that's really the only way we'll know."

Annalyla shook her head. "Nay, that is not it," she said. "I am not concerned with the fire in the hearth. There is something else."

Mawgwen pulled her head out of the hearth, her face red and sweaty. It was then that Maude asked Mercy to go and find the quartermaster and ask the man to come see to the blocked chimney to make sure it was in working order. When the young girl in the threadbare clothing fled the kitchen, they finally had the privacy they needed. Annalyla fixed on the old woman.

"I read the hide you gave me," she said. "It did, indeed, contain a message and I must ask you about it."

Mawgwen looked very interested. She pointed to the hide under Maude's arm. "What is it, milady?" she gasped. "The curse? Did it tell ye of the curse?"

Annalyla considered her reply carefully. "What do you know of the missing amulet?"

Mawgwen blinked; she was expecting an earth-shattering answer, not a question in return. She couldn't read, nor could any of her family, so she was hoping that someone who could read would tell her what the curse actually said. That had been part of her selfish hope in giving Lady de Velt the hide. But all she received was a question in response to her answer, and that displeased her.

"Only what I told ye, milady," she said. "It was taken from the wicked lord's wife and some think he searches for it."

Annalyla lifted an eyebrow. "You told me that your grandfather said that the ghost searches for it," she said. "You said it as if it was fact. Now you tell me that only *some* think he searches for it?"

Mawgwen looked back and forth between Maude and Annalyla, looking for some hint as to why they were asking these questions.

"No one knows for sure, of course," she said, considerably quieter. "Why do ye want to know about the amulet?"

"Because I want to know what *you* know of it," Annalyla said. She could sense that the woman was becoming guarded and that, coupled with the woman's attempt to convince her to flee Baiadepaura, didn't sit well with her. "Is that why you have come, Mawgwen? To look for this amulet? You said your ancestor was part of the mob that killed the last lord of Baiadepaura. You have also told me that the curse over Baiadepaura is now mine and that I must leave. *Why* do you want me to leave, Mawgwen? What are you not telling me?"

Mawgwen stiffened. "If ye don't want me here, then I can just as easily leave," she said, hastily turning for her possessions, which were still in the kitchen. "I won't stay if ye don't want me to."

She was picking up her things. Annalyla rushed at her, with Maude following a split second later. Together, they ganged up on the woman, grabbing her by the arms and forcing her to drop her possessions. Annalyla went so far as to shove the woman down onto a stone bench that was built into the wall of the kitchen.

"You are not going anywhere," Annalyla growled. "I want you to tell me what you know of the amulet. What more do you know about this place that you've not told me?"

Mawgwen put up her hands, fearful a slap would be coming her way. "Nothing, milady!" she cried. "I told ye everything I know. I brought ye the curse! I did that for yer protection!"

"Or did you do it to scare me?" Annalyla fired back. "I want you to tell me everything you know about this place and about the amulet. If you do not, I shall send for my husband and you'll not like it if he becomes involved. He is a very big man with a sword, Mawgwen. Will you answer my questions or do you wish to answer to my husband?"

Mawgwen was increasingly frightened. This was not how she'd imagined her stay at Baiadepaura would go. She'd expected to have some measure of dominance over the fearful army who knew nothing of the cursed castle. Instead, the lady of the castle wasn't an innocent lamb, but a shrewd woman who didn't believe everything she was told. That wasn't something Mawgwen had anticipated.

Her control was slipping.

"I will tell ye, milady," she said, her voice trembling. "If ye're asking about the amulet, no one knows what has become of it. My grandfather said that he was told that the man who stole it fell into the fire along with the wicked lord and his wife. If it left Baiadepaura, then it did not leave with him."

Annalyla eyed her suspiciously. "Then you do not have it?"

"Nay, milady, I swear it."

"And you've not come looking for it?"

Mawgwen shook her head firmly. "I've not, I swear," she said. "I only came to give ye the hide and tell ye how to leave the curse behind ye."

"And you have not heard if anyone has left with the amulet?"

"Nay, milady. I've not heard."

Annalyla still didn't believe her, but short of beating the woman, she wasn't sure how to get to the truth. Twice, a ghostly whisper had asked for Anyu's horse, so at least part of what Mawgwen had told her was true. At least, it was coming to make some sense now. But there was a very big piece of the puzzle missing.

"It has been two hundred years since the last lord of Baiadepaura was killed," she said. "What do you know of the men who have occupied this castle since then?"

Mawgwen lowered the hand she had in front of her face, the one meant to deflect the slaps she'd been anticipating. "Well," she said slowly, "after the wicked lord was killed, my grandfather said it remained vacant for a very long time. No one would come near it. When the villagers left the castle, they left it in shambles. The passage of time caused it to fall into ruin. Then, it belonged to Lords of St. Austell for a time, I heard. I think they're the ones who built some of the stone walls. The Lords of Truro took possession and they had men stationed here from time to time. When I was a *mos*, they were here, but they have not been here in many years."

"So there has never been steady occupation in all that time?"

"Nay, milady."

Annalyla looked at Maude. "Then mayhap, the tracks of what happened those years ago haven't been completely destroyed."

Maude looked at her curiously. "What do you mean?"

Annalyla had an idea. “Come with me.”

With that, she took Mawgwen by the arm and pulled her to her feet. Maude got in on the other side of the woman and, together, they forcibly escorted the old lady out of the kitchen and up the steps to the windy bailey. The clouds were blowing over now, puffy gray clouds against the backdrop of blue sky, and they could smell rain on the breeze.

A storm was coming.

But Annalyla intended to see her idea through before the rains came. Her mind was working on the amulet, and what had become of it, and she wanted to think it through. If the amulet had been lost or buried, she could do nothing. But perhaps, a logical process might help them figure out what had become of it.

Or not.

In any case, Annalyla took Mawgwen and Maude out into the bailey.

“Now,” Annalyla let go of the old woman just as they reached the approximate center of the bailey. “I was told that the wicked lord and his wife were burned to death.”

Mawgwen and Maude were standing together, nodding. “Aye, milady,” Mawgwen said. “This is true. A great fire consumed them.”

Annalyla nodded as she looked around the bailey. “Wouldn’t you think that if you’re going to kill someone, then you would do it where everyone could see it?”

Mawgwen looked to Maude in confusion, who was looking at Annalyla. “They are probably going to do it where you are standing,” she said. “There, in the middle of the bailey, so everyone could see. Why do you ask?”

Annalyla looked at the ground beneath her feet; hundreds of stones lined the bailey now and she knelt down, putting her fingers on the stones.

“Mawgwen, when was this bailey cobbled?” she asked. “This isn’t usual, you know. My husband said that the bailey was cobbled because they must have terrible trouble with the rains. The stones prevent the entire bailey from being washed away."

Mawgwen still wasn't sure what was going on, or why they were here, but she answered. "It must have been the Lords of Truro," she said. "They built bigger walls and they built on to the keep. I remember this because they took men from the village to work on the building. When I came here as a child with my grandmother, the cobblestones in the bailey were here."

Maude was listening to the old woman. When she finished speaking, she looked at Annalyla. "Why do you ask?" she said. "What are you thinking, Annie?"

Annalyla wasn't sure at the moment, but a definitive thought was taking form. "I was thinking that if this is where they burned the wicked lord, then from what I have been told, they simply left everything here. Ashes, bones, everything. Mawgwen, they did not clean up the mess, did they?"

Mawgwen shook her head. "Nay, milady," she said. "They did the deed and they fled."

Big, fat raindrops began to fall, pelting them as well as the stone. Mawgwen glanced up at the sky, unhappy that she was going to be rained on, but Annalyla didn't move. She was still looking at the bailey.

"So, they left everything behind," she said thoughtfully. "They left a pile of ashes and bones here and, presumably, the amulet that fell into the fire when the man who stole it was burned. So the amulet was here, buried in ash."

Maude lifted her eyebrows. "And?"

Annalyla looked at her as the rain began to fall harder as the heavens suddenly let loose. Men around the bailey were running for cover, but not the women. Very quickly, they were being soaked.

"*And* the ash had to go somewhere," she said. "Otherwise, the pile would still be standing here, so if no one cleaned it up over the years that the castle was vacant, it had to go somewhere."

Maude wiped the rain out of her eyes. "But where?"

Annalyla shook her head. "I suppose it would blow away," she said. "Or, with the amount of rain they seem to have here, mayhap, it was washed away."

That made the women take another look at the bailey, this time with more curiosity and consideration for the bailey as a whole. The answers to their questions were possibly here if they could only figure it out. The bailey was sloped slightly towards the keep and away from the hall. In fact, the entire bailey sloped towards the keep and the sea cliff beyond.

Then, they saw it.

As they watched, little rivers of rainwater began to trickle in the direction of the keep. Both Annalyla and Maude saw it and, at that moment, it was the only thing that had their attention. They began to follow the rainwater as it drained away from the very spot they surmised once held the funeral pyre for the wicked lord and his wife. As the rain continued to fall, soaking them both, they followed the water as it drained towards the west.

At one point, Maude took the hide, still under her arm, and buried it in her skirts so it wouldn't get terribly wet, but Annalyla was singularly focused on the flow of water. Her head was wet and water was dripping from her eyelashes. The three women followed it until the draining water ran right to the keep and then began draining into small vents that were at the base of the north wing of the keep.

The holes were small, cut into the foundation of the ground floor, but it occurred to Annalyla were the water was going. She looked up at Maude, who had the exact same thought, because the words out of their mouths at that moment matched entirely.

"The vault."

They said it at the same time. Without another word between them, they turned and ran for the stairs that led to the kitchens because the vaults were attached to the kitchen. Mawgwen followed, but at a distance. She didn't like what was happening with those women and she could see, clearly, that they were not going to leave Baiadepaura. Her attempts to force them to flee had no effect. In fact, Lady de Velt seemed suspicious of her motives and rather than be forced to tell why she'd really come, she thought it better to flee the castle and leave the occupants to their fates. The pirates would be there at dark and stubborn Lady de Velt would have to pay the price.

There was nothing more she could do.

Therefore, she hung back even as Lady de Velt and Lady de Correa charged through the small, fortified door to the vault that was just off the kitchen. She could hear them talking about needing light, and Lady de Correa came back into the kitchen to find something to fashion a torch with. All she found was an old broom, but she lit the bristles, anyway, and took it back into the vault with her.

Mawgwen could see the flicker of flame against the walls of the vault and she could hear the women speaking, but not their words. All she knew was that they were distracted and if there was ever a time for her to leave, it was now. Grabbing her possessions that were still against the wall of the old, dusty kitchen, she fled from the chamber, taking her crow with her, who had been making itself at home beneath an old Davey Elm tree.

Slipping from Baiadepaura through the nearly-repaired portcullis, old Mawgwen left the castle and the ladies to their fates, and fled into the countryside, never to be seen or heard from again.

CHAPTER FOURTEEN

THE BROOM HADN'T lasted long.

In fact, it burned quickly, and smoked heavily, and gave off very little light, forcing Annalyla and Maude to leave the vault and go to the hall to find the oil lamps that the quartermaster had brought with him. He also brought fat tallow tapers, a precious sack of them, along with iron sconces that would light halls and chambers and tables. While Maude distracted him, Annalyla stole four tapers and an iron sconce that happened to have four arms with spiked tips. As she whisked out of the hall, trying to keep the tapers dry for the trek across the bailey, Maude excused herself from the confused quartermaster and followed.

Now, they had light. With the four tapers lit from the kitchen hearth and settled on the sconce, Maude carried it into the vault. The candles gave off a great deal of light and the old, musty-smelling vault was bathed in a faint glow. It was also a wet vault, as the floor of it was puddled with runoff from the storm. And they could see that the vents that faced the bailey had all of that runoff water draining right into the vault.

But that wasn't all they saw.

Decades and even centuries of neglect were evident. There seemed to be stores there, still, left over from the last occupants, but they were on the southwest side of the vault and raised on stones to keep them off of the muddy ground. The only thing on the eastern side of the vault, where all of the water and runoff from the bailey was coming in, was a sea of debris from decades and decades of rain runoff. All of it was washed into the vault from a very poorly designed drainage system in the bailey.

"Look at all of this," Maude muttered, looking at the piles and piles of debris. "It looks like a burial vault in here with all of that wet earth."

Annalyla couldn't disagree. "But the neglect of this vault, and the castle, might be our good fortune," she said. "If no one has cleaned this mess in two centuries, or longer, then the chances of us finding the amulet might be good."

Maude shook her head. "Do you really believe that?"

"It is possible," Annalyla insisted, although she wasn't really sure. "If the amulet was washed out of the bailey from the years of rain, and ended up here in the vault, then we will find it."

"More than likely, someone has already found it and made off with it."

"We will not know unless we try."

Maude looked at Annalyla, distress on her face. "How, Annie?" she wanted to know. "There is so much debris here. It will take days or months or even years to dig this all up."

Annalyla was trying not to feel discouraged as she looked at the wet pile that was getting wetter by the moment. She looked at the runoff of water to see where it was going, trying to decide if it was better to walk away.

But something in her refused to give up.

Rushing back into the kitchen, she could see old iron implements near the hearth, including a big shovel used to scoop out the ashes. She grabbed it and ran back into the vault, eyeing the piles of mud and debris.

"Look," she said to Maude. "Most of the water is coming from that big vent, the one we could see in the bailey. If something came through that vent, and it was heavy enough, don't you think that it would fall straight to the ground and not move? It would be buried by the earth coming in after it."

Maude shrugged; she was intimidated by the task Annalyla wanted to undertake. "Possibly," she said. "Annie, let's simply tell Tenner about this. He should know, anyway, considering this is his castle. Show him the hide and tell him what Mawgwen told us. Mayhap, he will help us dig this up."

Annalyla shook her head. "He does not believe in ghosts," she said. "He has told me so. How can I tell him that I saw a ghost today, not once, but twice?"

"He will believe because I was there, too. I saw it at least once."

Annalyla sighed heavily. "He will think we are hysterical women. I only just married the man, Maude. I do not wish for him to think he has married a fool."

Maude could understand her position. "Is that why you have not told him any of this?"

Annalyla didn't say anything for a moment. When she finally did, her tone was soft. "Our marriage was almost over before it started," she said. "Tenner and I have had to endure some unpleasantries, and now we are at a place where things are calm and kind between us. I do not wish to disrupt that with talk of a ghost, Maude. He will think me daft."

Maude reached out, putting a hand on her shoulder. "He will not think so," she said. "I have seen the way he looks at you, Annie. There is something in his expression I have never seen before. Tenner is a man of deep feeling, though he does not wish for anyone to know that. But I have known him for four years. I have seen his compassionate and understanding side."

"You have?" Annalyla looked up at her. "Tell me of this husband I have. I have never asked you to tell me anything, so do not speak on him if you feel it will betray a confidence. But you have known Tenner far longer than I. He speaks so highly of you."

Maude smiled. "It is not betraying a confidence to tell you that you have married a man of character and quality," she said. "I suppose the best example of compassion that I can give, that I witnessed, is when

Lady Jane injured her head. As the days and weeks passed, it was increasingly clear that she would not recover. Her betrothed, Beau, is a close friend of Tenner's. While Ivor was cruel in breaking the betrothal with Beau, Tenner showed a great deal of compassion about it. Beau and Jane were in love, you see, and Tenner knew it. He snuck Beau into the keep so he could say farewell to Jane, even though she was not in her right mind at the time. But Tenner made sure that Beau and Jane said their farewells. He was quite sad for Beau."

Annalyla smiled faintly. "He did not tell me that," she said. "He told me about Beau and Lady Jane and how sad he was because Beau was his friend, but he did not tell me the lengths he went to so that they could be together."

"I fear that Tenner de Velt is a secret romantic."

Annalyla laughed softly. "He would be the rarest of all creatures if he was," she said. "Even so, he showed great understanding in the situation."

"And he will show great understanding with you," Maude said firmly. "You do not give him enough credit for his response. He will be reasonable."

Annalyla sighed. "Very well," she said after a moment. "I shall take your advice. But first, let me dig around a little. Just to satisfy my own curiosity."

Maude wouldn't stop her. She held the tapers closer to the pile directly under the main vent. "Dig at will," she said. "Mayhap there is something there worth finding."

Annalyla got a good grip on the shovel. Trying to keep the hem of her surcoat out of the mud, which was a fairly impossible task, she began to hack at the debris right under the main vent where water was still pouring in. In fact, the water softened the debris, which came apart with surprising ease. It was very wet, and moldy, and smelled terrible once she started breaking it apart. But she hacked at it, loosening it up and shoveling it away, as Maude stood there and held out the light with one hand, pinching her nose with the other.

The more Annalyla plowed into the dirt with the old iron shovel, the more determined she seemed to become. She was almost frantic in her movements, poking and chopping with the shovel one moment, then scooping up dirt the next and tossing it into another pile.

Soon, decades of earth began to fall away. There were leaves from the old Davey Elm tree outside, and sometimes they would come across nails from a horse's shoe. They discovered more than one decomposing rat, which Annalyla tossed away with disgust. They found shoes, spoons, and even a dagger. So much debris as Annalyla carved away the layers of time, looking for a lost amulet that probably wasn't even there. But she had to try; for the sake of a man who had been wrongly killed, she felt very strongly she had to try.

"Maude," she said as she hacked away at a section just beneath the vent. "Did you know Arlo before you married him?"

Maude nodded her head. "Aye," she said. "I met Arlo when we were both fostering at Berkeley Castle."

"And you knew you loved him when you met him?"

Maude grinned. "Mayhap not at the first, but certainly shortly thereafter," she said. "I wrote to my father and told him that I wanted to marry him. It was my father who then offered Arlo a betrothal."

"And he took it right away?"

"He took it gladly."

Annalyla paused. "I have been thinking what it must have been like to have loved a man and watched him die," she said, her movements with the shovel slowing. "The woman, Anyu, who wore the horse amulet had to watch her husband die. I cannot imagine what madness I would feel if I had to watch Tenner die."

Maude sobered. "It must have been horror beyond belief," she said softly. "I would pray for death as well if Arlo was killed before me."

Annalyla resumed chopping away at the hardened earth. "I suppose that is why this is important to me," she said. "I have a new husband. I am not ashamed to say that I adore him. But for Anyu and Faustus, they were helpless against the people that killed them. It is not fair."

"Nay, it is not."

"And the ghost… he wants what belonged to his wife and I feel strongly that I must find it for him. Now that I have experienced such happiness… I cannot explain it better than that. I must help him."

Maude watched her as she hacked away at the mud, tossing aside shovelfuls of it. Looking around, she found a place to perch the sconce on a dividing wall near the middle of the vault.

"I shall find something to dig with and help you," she said quietly. "Mayhap, we will find what we need to find faster."

Annalyla smiled gratefully at her as the woman disappeared into the kitchen and returned with a long iron spit, one used to roast meat over the open fire. As she used the sharp end to hack into the mud, Annalyla shoveled it away. Maude would loosen and Annalyla would shovel it away.

They went on like that for quite some time. In fact, the tapers began to burn lower, which told them they'd been at it at least a couple of hours. Annalyla's arms told her much the same; they were beginning to ache. Maude moved over to a rather deep hole that Annalyla had dug out earlier, one that was almost directly beneath the vent, and began jamming the iron rod into the sides of it to break up more mud. Annalyla scooped up a shovelful of earth and as she dumped it in the corner with the rest of the softened dirt, something caught her eye.

Setting the shovel aside, she knelt down, pawing through the dark, wet earth until she came to what she'd seen. It was small and white, and as she brushed the dirt away, she quickly realized what it was.

Part of a tooth.

Horror and shock swept her, but she kept her head. "Maude?" she said. "Come quickly."

Maude hustled over the slippery mud until she came to Annalyla's side, kneeling down next to her. "What is it?"

Swallowing hard, Annalyla held up the object. "Look."

Maude took it and she, too, paled when she realized what it was. "God's Bones," she hissed. "A tooth."

Annalyla nodded. "Do… do teeth burn?"

Maude shrugged, looking to the area she had just come from. "I do not know," she said honestly. "Let us see what else is in there."

It was a gruesome thought, but Annalyla followed Maude back over to the pit that was directly below the vent. The two of them got down onto their knees, resigned to the fact that they were dirty and muddy, and began to dig around in the pit with their fingers. They became even dirtier and muddier. At one point, Maude went to retrieve the tapers so they would have better light in the depths of the hole.

Then, they began to see all sorts of things.

Pieces of burned wood and mud that smelled faintly of rot. The exact scent was difficult to describe. They were pulling out a great deal of burned wood, setting it aside and then digging down for more. Annalyla then began pulling out pieces of something hard, something she wasn't quite sure what it was until one of them had a knuckle on the end. Sickened, she handed it to Maude, who looked equally distressed.

"It's a bone," Maude said softly.

"It could be an animal bone," Annalyla suggested.

Maude nodded and set the bone aside, but they both knew that the chances of it being an animal bone were slim. It made their stomachs roll, but they couldn't stop now. They were on to something. They began pulling out more and more pieces of bone, some of it large, some of it small, setting it all aside. When Maude began digging at something stuck in the earth, trying to dig around it, both she and Annalyla realized that it was the round part of a skull.

They stopped.

Maude stood up and moved away, feeling ill and frightened, but Annalyla couldn't give up. Without saying a word, she found her shovel again and started to dig again. She dug furiously, her hair falling over her face, sweat beading on her brow. She was possessed with her determination to find something of legend, something that had belonged to a woman once loved by a man who was wrongly killed.

Perhaps it was all madness; perhaps she would never find it. But she wasn't prepared for that. Had this situation, or this legend, become known before she married Tenner, maybe she wouldn't feel so determined to find what, perhaps, could not be found. But all she could think of was the writing on the hide, and how Faustus de Paura spoke of his dear Anyu. He had loved the woman; Annalyla could sense it. She could *feel* it. All of the legends and curses in the world couldn't speak to her heart the way a few small words on brittle hide had.

Now that she had married Tenner, and now that she understood what it meant to be consumed with someone, she felt great pity and compassion for Faustus and Anyu, and the wrongs committed against them. Death had separated them, yet Faustus was still at Baiadepaura, still lingering. If it was because of the amulet, then Annalyla wanted to help him. Perhaps, that was what was really behind all of this… now, she understood what it was to love someone for, in truth, she loved Tenner.

She couldn't remember when she hadn't.

It wasn't even a startling revelation; the thought entered her mind gently and she accepted it, as natural as anything on earth. She loved the man, and all was right in the world. Therefore, all she could think of was what it would be like to have been cruelly separated from Tenner, watching him die and being unable to help him. The very idea ate at her, so that was why finding the amulet – if it even existed – was so important to her. In fact, there were tears in her eyes as she chopped and dug, shoveling out dirt until her arms were sore and shaking.

Shovelfuls of bones came out, and the partial skull that had been buried in the mud. As horrifying as it was, she pushed past the horror of it, aiming for the ultimate goal. She set everything aside in a careful pile, keeping it all together, and soon enough, Maude rejoined her, helping her dig a little more. But time was passing, and the tapers were burning lower. Maude's soft voice finally filled the air.

"Annie," she said. "It is time to stop. We have many other things to do, including an evening meal to oversee, and this will simply have to wait. Annie? Do you understand me?"

Annalyla did. Gradually, she slowed down, but only because her arms were badly aching. She could hardly raise the shovel any longer. Discouraged, and saddened, she sat down next to the pit, looking down into the darkness of it and seeing that more water from the rain was trickling into it. Soon enough, the pit would fill again. All of her work would be for naught. Wiping at the tears on her face with the back of her hand, she set the shovel down.

"I so wanted to find it," she whispered tightly. "I wanted to help this ghost, this man, who has waited two hundred years to find a part of his wife he has been missing all of these years."

Maude looked at the pile of bones against the wall where they had carefully placed the piles. "But I think we found *him*, and that is something," she said gently. "What you have done today is very noble, but it is time to tell Tenner. Show him the hide. Tell him what we found down here. Those bones deserve a Christian burial."

Annalyla nodded, turning to look at the bones as well. "They must be Faustus and his wife," she said. "Don't you think? They were washed down here by the years of rains, the only pieces left of them after being burned to death. I wonder… I wonder if we do not find the amulet, if the ghost will be satisfied that we've found his bones? Mayhap he'll be satisfied if we bury him."

Maude could only shake her head. "I do not know," she whispered. "I hope so. Come along, sweetheart. Get up. Let us find Tenner and tell him our story."

Resigned and saddened, Annalyla nodded. She passed once last glance at the pit as she prepared to rise and, as she did so, something glistened in the weak candlelight. Curious, she reached her hand down into the pit. There was something shiny sticking out of the side of the hole, partially uncovered, and she put her fingers on it, trying to pull it out. It didn't come easily, so she dug around it with her fingertips, finally able to pull it out.

It was something gold.

But the gold was dark and twisted, and Annalyla looked at it curiously. In fact, Maude saw it, too, and she held up the iron sconce so they could both get a better look at it.

"What is it?" Maude asked.

Annalyla shook her head. "I am not sure," she said. It was caked with mud so she splashed it around in the runoff water to wash it off. Then, she held it up again. "It is gold, whatever it is, but it looks broken, like part of it has been destroyed. It is twisted and..."

She suddenly stopped and her eyes widened as she rubbed her fingers across the gold, trying to clean out the little grooves that were caked with dirt. She rubbed it on her skirts, cleaning it further, before holding it up into the light again. Then, her face lit up when she saw what looked like half of a horse's face.

"Look!" she said, excitement filling her tone. "Maude, it's a horse's face! I see a nose, an eye, and an ear. Do you see it?"

Maude grabbed it from her, holding it next to the candlelight. Her eyes widened and her jaw dropped as she, too, saw what looked very much like a horse's head.

"My God," she gasped. "It... it *does* look like a horse's head. I cannot believe it!"

"It's the amulet!" Annalyla cried. "Maude, *it's the amulet*!"

Maude could hardly believe it. "Is it possible?" she breathed, looking at the pit they'd been digging in with utter astonishment. "Is it really possible that we found it in all of this mess and madness?"

Annalyla was almost delirious with joy. "What else could it be?"

Maude was trying to be logical, but it was difficult. "A coin," she said. "A charm. A man's charm? Men carry pieces for luck, you know."

Annalyla refused to believe that they'd found anything other than what they'd been looking for. She began to laugh with excitement.

"It is Anyu's horse," she insisted. "It is, I know it!"

Maude wasn't sure what to believe anymore. "It does *not* look like an amulet," she said. "It is broken and twisted, and it does not look as if it belonged to a woman."

Annalyla was still staring at the horse's head. "If it fell into a fire, then the fire would soften the metal, wouldn't it?" she said. "Mayhap, the fire damaged it. It is only a small piece of something, but how could it be anything else other than the amulet? We found it with the pile of bones that have char marks on them!"

Maude didn't have an answer to that. Annalyla's excitement was catching and she reached out with her dirty hands, pulling Annalyla to her feet.

"Come on," she said. "We must find Tenner. The man needs to know what is happening, Annie. We can no longer keep it from him."

Annalyla was the first to agree. She no longer had any fear of telling Tenner about the hide, and the ghost, and most of all, the horsehead amulet, not when she had the proof in her hands. In fact, she was more than eager to tell him.

With the broken amulet tucked into her dirty palm, she was the first one out of the vault and through the kitchen, racing for the keep to tell her husband what she had discovered. Perhaps, the curse of Baiadepaura was about to be lifted once and for all. And perhaps, a wandering ghost was to finally know satisfaction.

She could only hope that was true.

CHAPTER FIFTEEN

"I TOLD YOU that I do not believe in ghosts or curses."

Those were the first words out of Tenner's mouth as Annalyla and Maude faced him in the master's chamber that faced south, overlooking the turbulent sea. For Annalyla, who had raced into the chamber so gleefully to tell him what she'd discovered, his words were like a punch to the gut.

"But…" she said, shocked. "But Maude told you what she saw. I saw it, too. We both heard it. And we have been digging in the vault all afternoon. We found burned bones and we found this – the amulet."

Tenner had been roused out of a heavy sleep by his excited and filthy wife. He hadn't been perturbed about it until he'd been told the reason why she'd awoken him. Now, he was annoyed, with her and with Maude. Silly, giddy women. His sleepy gaze moved between the two of them as Annalyla extended the piece of dark gold, but he didn't take it from her. He simply glanced at it.

"So you have been digging in the vault," he said coldly. "You dug through decades and centuries of rubbish and God knows what else. The legends of this place have gotten into your heads, so you found rubbish and created a story with it. That is all."

Annalyla dropped her hand, the one holding the gold piece. Feeling ashamed and scolded, she turned to Maude, who was holding the hide. She took it from the woman and unrolled it, trying to hand it to her stubborn husband.

"Read this, please," she begged softly. "It was given to me by a woman whose grandfather's grandfather was part of the mob that killed the last lord of Baiadepaura. This was written by the man they call the wicked lord – please see what it says. Then you will understand that it is not a legend that we have succumbed to, but a tragedy. He was not a devil, but a man who was greatly wronged. It is a wrong that must be righted."

Tenner eyed the hide, but he didn't take it from her. In fact, his jaw began to tick and he turned away from the pair, rubbing the sleep from his eyes.

"Let me tell you what you have fallen victim to," he said. "You have already heard the legend. It was in your heads when you came to Baiadepaura. Maude, I expected better from you, but Annalyla… the truth is that we have not known each other that long. I thought you were a rational creature, but it is clear that you are young and still impressionable. You have both fallen victim to the legend of this place, and you are reading things into objects and missives that are not there. There are no ghosts and there is no curse, and whatever is on that hide has nothing to do with this place."

Now, Maude felt as if her integrity was also under attack. "Tenner, you are being unfair," she said steadily. "The hide is very old, given to us by a woman from the village. She has come here to serve in the kitchens. The hide has been in her family since the last lord of Baiadepaura was killed. The missive is signed by a man named de Paura, and he speaks of the sickness that plagued the area. He begs for mercy and compassion, and he writes of being unable to speak. It is clear that the man was not wicked and that he was blamed for something that was not his doing. And he further speaks of his dear Anyu, his wife. It is the same thing we heard earlier when the ghost spoke to us."

Tenner looked at her. Then, he shook his head. "Maude," he said. "Listen to yourself – this is not the same reasonable woman I have known all these years."

Maude stood her ground. “Because this *happened*,” she said, raising her voice because he was being so stubborn. “Do you truly think we would run in here and spout off foolery to you if it had not happened? Your wife even expressed her fears in telling you because she did not want you to think her daft. It was I who insisted we tell you.”

Tenner was shaking her head before she even finished. “I forgive you both,” he said. “You are weary. This has been a taxing journey and we are in a terrible place. How could it not affect you? But I will tell you what has happened – a woman from the village has given you a forgery, a missive with words that confirm the legend so that she can tell you stories and you will depend upon her.”

“That is not true!”

“Isn’t it?” Tenner fired back softly. “Tell me something, Maude; where did you find this alleged amulet? And where did you find the bones?”

Maude was trying very hard not to become angry. “We told you. In the vault.”

“And where is the vault?”

“Down below the ground level of the keep.”

He nodded impatiently. “And what is attached to the vault?”

“What do you mean?”

“What chamber is attached to the vault?”

Maude understood. “The kitchen.”

“And you said this woman was a kitchen servant?”

“Aye.”

“Did you ever leave her alone in the kitchen?”

Maude paused a moment, thinking that she knew what he was about to say. It infuriated her. “We did,” she said steadily. “I was in the hall with some of our new servants and Annie took the hide from the woman. She left the old woman alone in the kitchen when she went to read the hide.”

Tenner cocked a dark eyebrow as he looked at his pale, dirty wife. “And you do not think the woman could have planted this amulet and even the bones in the vault while you were away?"

Annalyla shook her head. "It is not possible," she said. "We had to dig through a good deal of dirt to find those things."

"And you would be willing to swear on your life that the hide you were given is not a forgery?"

Annalyla had enough. This was the reaction she'd feared from Tenner, only she hadn't imagined it would be so vicious. He was angry, and tired, and completely unlike the man she'd come to know over the past few days. She was feeling belittled and beaten, and utterly ashamed.

"Nay," she said after a moment. "I am not willing to swear on my life that it is not a forgery. But I know what I saw and heard; I saw a ghost. I heard him say *Anyu equi.* I *will* swear on my life to that, and whether or not you believe me, it is the truth. I thought I was bringing something of importance to you, because you are an understanding and reasonable man, but it is clear that understanding and reason does not pertain to me. I am terribly sorry to have troubled you, my lord, for it will not happen again. Forgive me if I have made you ashamed of me. Now, if you will excuse me, I have duties to attend to."

With that, she turned away, rushing out of the chamber before anyone could stop her. She bolted past Maude on her way out and Maude saw her face crumpling, tears in her eyes. When the door slammed behind her, Maude turned to Tenner.

"This is my fault," she said hoarsely. "I convinced her that you were kind and understanding, and that you would listen to what she had discovered, but I was wrong. You had no right and no reason to behave that way towards her, Tenner. Annie is a sweet woman, and very bright, and all she wants to do is please you. Do you know what she told me in the vault as she was digging up the bones? She told me that she adored you. She told me that she could not imagine watching you perish in front her, as the last lord of Baiadepaura perished in front of his wife. She did it because of what she feels for you."

Some of the hardness went out of Tenner's expression. "Maude..."

She cut him off, sternly. "Nay," she said. "You will not explain yourself to me, for nothing excuses what I just witnessed. Annie told me that the reason she wants to help this ghost, this searching ghost, is because she understands his anguish now that she has experienced such happiness with you. And you treat her this way? I am ashamed of you, Tenner de Velt. Even if you did not believe her, you did not have to be so cruel about it."

More of Tenner's hardness faded and he sighed heavily, turning away. "What you two expect me to believe is not logical. I cannot base my command on ghosts and rumors. Did you truly expect me to believe it?"

Maude shook her head. "Believe what you will," she said. "But do not call us liars, for we are not. If you do not trust us any more than that, then mayhap it was a mistake in coming here. Mayhap we should return to Seven Crosses. Your logic can be your chatelaine and keep you warm at night. At least you will not have hysterical women underfoot."

With that, she stormed out of the chamber also, slamming the door behind her and leaving Tenner feeling depressed and remorseful. There was great truth to Maude's words, and he knew she was right about the way he'd been cruel to Annalyla – he had been. He was usually in better control of his emotions, but the cruelty sprang from the fact that he realized, as he heard her talk about seeing a ghost, that he was disappointed. Disappointed that she didn't think like him and act like him in all things.

It was true that they barely knew one another. He'd seen a witty, kind, and intelligent woman over the past few days, a woman he was obsessed with on many levels. They laughed at the same things and seemed to have common likes and dislikes, and she was very eager to please him. What was it he'd called her at the start? An honest woman. It was the most important thing to him aside from loyalty. Now, he'd just called that honest woman a liar. A fool, even. He was disappointed that she'd given credence to a legend.

But now, it was his turn to feel like a fool.

He hadn't meant to hurt her.

Turning around, he noticed that the old hide was on the end of the bed where Annalyla had set it. It drew his eye and as much as he didn't even want to look at it, he found that he couldn't look away. Before he realized it, he was picking it up and looking at the faded brown writing, words in Latin that he could understand.

He read the missive, twice. He noted the signature at the bottom, looking very much like de Paura, just as Annalyla had said. The message itself was rather sad, and tragic, and went completely against the legends he'd been told. It wasn't a curse or the words of an angry man, a but rather tragic and poignant message. In spite of himself, he was interested in it.

His thoughts kept going back to what Maude had said, about Annalyla finding happiness with him. She adored him. In fact, that seemed to be the only thing he wanted to focus on because his feelings were very much the same. He was soft-hearted, and compassionate, but it was fear that kept those things buried for the most part beneath a ramrod iron façade, the consummate knight. Fear because men in this day and age viewed compassion or emotion as a woman's trait, and in a man, it could be viewed as weakness.

He wasn't weak; he was a de Velt, and the House of de Velt had a dark and terrible history up until a few decades ago. His grandfather, Ajax de Velt, had been a horrible and brutal man in his youth, killing men in a most horrific way in his conquest. But that had all changed when he'd met Tenner's grandmother. Still, the indiscretions of his youth were things that continued to cast a shadow over the de Velt name, so if men knew that the grandson of Ajax de Velt was compassionate and emotional, it would further damage the de Velt name.

Therefore, Tenner spent a good deal of time putting up a front. A hard and decisive and logical front. But Maude had seen through it, and so had Arlo. He trusted them. But Annalyla… she'd seen that side of him, too. He hadn't really minded until he realized how much he felt for her and, then, it was as if he'd let her see his weakness. She *was* his weakness. Perhaps, he was simply ashamed to tell her.

But, perhaps, he needed to.

With a heavy sigh, Tenner set the old hide aside and went to find his boots. Still in the tunic and leather breeches he slept in, he found his boots at the end of the bed and tied them on, running his fingers through his long hair as he headed from the chamber.

He had a wife to find.

OLD MAWGWEN WASN'T anywhere to be found, but Mercy was hard at work in the kitchen of Baiadepaura as she prepared bread dough. She'd even lit up the old kiln in the kitchen yard outside, even though it was raining heavily, and as Annalyla descended the stairs to the kitchen, she could see the kiln smoking furiously.

Entering the kitchen, it was warm and smelled of smoke, and Mercy was very busy. Annalyla was trying to push aside what had happened with Tenner and focus on what needed to be done for the coming meal. All of the stores had been brought to the kitchen, so she knew she had salted beef and other things to work with, but she needed to find Mawgwen. She needed the help.

With Mercy busy on the bread, Annalyla went through the barrels and sacks lining the wall and into the vault, which were dry of any moisture. The flooding seemed to be isolated on the eastern side of the vault. But entering the vault reminded her of Tenner again, and of the golden horsehead in her pocket. She thought of the bones that she and Maude had discovered, feeling sick to her stomach that Tenner thought it was all a lie. The reaction was everything she had feared from him, and more.

And it was her fault.

She shouldn't have told him. She shouldn't have listened to Maude and kept it all to herself. The man had so much to worry about without her coming to him with tales of ghosts and curses. Once she calmed down and stopped weeping, she would apologize to him and hope he forgave her. She hoped he didn't think she was the village idiot, running around spouting tales of ghosts. Whatever damage she'd done, she would work very hard to repair it.

She couldn't stand the thought of the man thinking he'd married a lunatic.

There was clean water in a bucket that Mercy had brought in, and Annalyla rinsed the dirt from her hands and face with it, splashing the water on her skin until it came clean. She didn't have any soap, so it would have to do for the time being. Drying her face and arms off with her skirt, she returned to the stores with the intention of beginning the meal preparation when she heard a quiet voice near the kitchen door.

"Annie."

It was Tenner. Startled, she looked up to see him blocking out most of the light from the doorway, his big frame filling it up. Apprehensive of his presence, she faced him, still drying off her hands.

"Aye, my lord?"

Tenner hesitated and Annalyla saw him look to Mercy, who was busily kneading dough, before returning his attention to her. "Would you come with me, please?"

The question indicated that he was unwilling to speak before witnesses and Annalyla didn't hesitate. She followed him out into the rain and he pulled her beneath the Davey Elm tree because the branches offered some shelter from the downpour. Annalyla's stomach was in knots as Tenner came to a pause and turned to her.

"Forgive me," he said simply. "I was unnecessarily unkind to you and I ask your forgiveness. I have no excuse other than talk of ghosts and curses and things I cannot touch or see frustrates me. I simply cannot believe in things that lesser men put stock in."

An apology was not what Annalyla had expected, even though the apology itself suggested he still thought she was a fool for believing in such things. He was just trying to be nice about it this time. Therefore, she was guarded. To be truthful, she was also hurt. Deeply hurt. But she nodded her head in response, averting her gaze.

"You will forgive me if I shamed you with such talk," she said rather stiffly. "Is that all, my lord?"

Tenner's gaze lingered on her. "It is *not* all," he said. "And do not address me formally. We are beyond such things. Annie, I am sorry I became angry. I should not have done that, and I should not have belittled you. I suppose… I suppose that sometimes I try so hard to be reasonable that it clouds my ability to see things beyond the limit of my understanding. You said you saw a ghost; I did not see it. I *have* not seen it. Therefore, to me, it does not exist."

Her head came up, her big eyes fixed on him. "But *I* saw it," she said quietly. "I saw it twice. It spoke both times. Do you truly believe I would lie to you about such things?"

He was trying not to become frustrated again. "Nay," he said. "But there is something else in what you said; I read the hide you left behind. I saw where whoever wrote the missive spoke of the inability to speak. If the last lord of Baiadepaura is this ghost, then how can he speak? The man who wrote the missive did not have that ability."

He had a point, but Annalyla knew what she'd heard. "Perhaps he had not a voice, but he could move his lips," she said. Then, she whispered the words without using her voice. "We are able to speak without using sound and volume. That is what I heard, my lord. A sound without volume, as if it was breathed into my ear."

Tenner didn't want to fight with her. He really didn't. Perhaps, he needed to put aside his unreasonable logic and listen to her. She hadn't lied to him since he'd known her, his truthful little wife, and he'd respected her greatly from the beginning because of it. He needed to stop being so narrow-minded and have faith in that trust they had established.

Have faith in *her*.

"Will you tell me what happened, then?" he asked sincerely. "Tell me everything from the beginning and I will listen without judgement, I promise."

Annalyla sighed reluctantly, afraid dredging up what she'd already told him would bring about another quarrel. But she indulged him.

"There is not much more to tell than I already told you," she said. "The old woman who had come from the village along with several other women to be employed as servants gave me the hide, and told me that her ancestor had taken it from Baiadepaura the same day that the wicked lord, the last lord, was killed. She told me it was a curse written by the lord himself and told me that we should leave immediately because of it. But when I read the hide, it was not a curse. If you read it, then you know what it says. It is a man begging for his life."

Tenner nodded faintly. "I know."

Annalyla continued. "When I read the hide, I was in the big chamber that faces out over the bailey, the one you have claimed as your solar," she said. "I read it several times before finally reading aloud as if it would help me understand the words better. And that is when I saw it."

"What?"

She thought hard, trying to describe exactly what she saw. "It was a mist," she said. "That is the only way I can describe it. It was as if a mist was inside the solar and as I watched, it took on the form of a man. And a hand touched me from this mist. It was so cold that it felt like ice, and then I heard the words *Anyu equi*."

Tenner remembered the words on the old hide. "My dear Anyu," he murmured. "I will assume that is his wife."

Annalyla nodded, perhaps warming a little to the conversation now that he wasn't ridiculing her. "That is my assumption as well," she said. "He said *Anyu equi* twice, to me when I was alone, and then also when Maude read it. It is part of what old Mawgwen said – she, too, spoke of the horsehead amulet that the wicked lord had given his wife. She said that is why he lingers, to find the amulet."

"Who is old Mawgwen?"

"The servant who gave me the hide."

"And that is why you went looking for it? Because the ghost said so?"

Annalyla nodded, trying not to feel stupid as he studied her. "Because of that, and because of the message on the hide," she said. "And... and the fact that the message has nothing to do with a curse, but everything to do with a man pleading for mercy. It's so tragic, Tenner. The poor man could not speak, so he wrote a missive to villagers who were too ignorant to read it. They killed him and he was innocent."

Tenner could see the distress on her brow and it was difficult not to feel some compassion for the situation. Even if he didn't believe it, she clearly did, and that touched him. She was a woman of great feeling and that was rare. He'd seen enough selfish women in his lifetime to know that. Faintly, he sighed.

"If that is what happened, then it is, indeed, a tragedy," he said. "So you went looking for this amulet."

She lifted her slender shoulders. "I did, but I did not truly think I would find anything."

"Why the vault?"

Annalyla explained about her theory about the location of the pyre where de Paura was killed. She also told him of the man who had stolen the amulet and had then promptly fallen into the fire himself to be burned alive along with the wicked lord. She explained about the rain, and how the water flowed into the vault, and the mess of debris that was there.

It all sounded very logical and, in truth, Tenner was rather impressed with the way her mind worked. She *was* logical, and reasonable, even if she was young and emotional. But the more she spoke, the guiltier he felt for having rejected her quest so easily. He could see that it meant a good deal to her, a woman who was trying to do good. When she was finished, he held out his hand to her.

"Let me see what you found," he said. "I am curious to see if it really is a horse's head."

Now that he was actually listening to her, Annalyla was eager to show him. She dug it out of her pocket and placed it in his palm, standing very close to him as he inspected it. In fact, they both inspected it as she pointed out that, although the piece was twisted and lumpy, the shape of the horse's head was unmistakable. He turned it over a few times, looking at it from all angles.

"And you found this in the vault?" he asked.

She nodded. "Maude and I dug it up," she said. "And the bones… they are human bones, Tenner."

"How do you know for certain?"

"Because we found part of a skull." She looked at him sadly. "They are charred, which lends credence to the stories of the wicked lord being burned to death. I think… I think we found him, Tenner. The poor man needs to be properly buried."

Tenner looked at the twisted gold piece a moment longer before handing it back to her. "The event you speak of happened two hundred years ago," he said. "Are you saying that no one has buried the man yet in all those years? That his bones are in a pile of rubbish in the vault?"

She nodded firmly. "Mawgwen told me that after the villagers killed the lord, Baiadepaura was vacant for a very long time," she said. "She did not say how long, but mayhap long enough for the rains to wash the bones and debris into the vault. Mayhap no one even knew they were there. We found them buried under quite a bit of mud. Would you like to see, Tenner?"

He could hear the hope in her voice. He had a dozen things to do at the moment, but none of them seemed as important as what Annalyla wanted. Considering how he'd behaved, he was eager to make amends. Smiling, he nodded his head.

"I think I'd better," he said.

Annalyla smiled in return, feeling a great deal of relief that things were forgiven between them. He held out his hand to her and she took it. Tenner began leading her towards the kitchen entry when they caught sight of people coming down the stairs towards the kitchen. As they stepped out from beneath the elm, they could see that Maude, Arlo, and Graham were on the approach.

Annalyla was glad to see them until she realized that Maude was looking rather angrily at Tenner. Quickly, she spoke.

"Tenner wishes to see where we have been digging," she said to the woman. "He has inspected the amulet and agrees that it looks like a horsehead."

Maude wasn't in a forgiving mood. "I see," she said. "Is that *all* he said?"

Tenner knew what she meant. He went to the woman and kissed her on the forehead. "I said that I was sorry," he told her. "I have begged forgiveness for acting like an arse and my lady has graciously forgiven me. I hope you will, too."

Because Maude and Tenner were such good friends, it didn't take much for Maude to forgive him, either. Reluctantly, she smiled.

"Oh, very well," she said. "I never could stay angry with you for very long."

Arlo, beside his wife, was looking between the two. "What's he done now?"

Maude waved him off. "Nothing of note," she said. "Come along; do you want to see the bones or not?"

The answer was unanimous.

CHAPTER SIXTEEN

"THOSE ARE MOST definitely human bones," Graham said distastefully. "God, what more of a mess will we find beneath all of this mud? There has to be centuries of mud and debris from the bailey in here."

The men were looking at the pile of bones that the women had carefully set aside. Maude had re-lit what remained of the candles they'd stolen from the quartermaster to inspect what seemed to be a graveyard beneath the keep. Arlo was over inspecting the vents where water from the storm outside was still pouring in, creating rivers and mud all around the east side of the vault.

"We will need to block off these vents, Ten," he said. "Once the weather clears, we'll send men in here with stones and mortar to block it up. I cannot imagine why it was not done years ago."

Tenner was crouched down, looking at the partial and charred skull that his wife had found. "From what I have seen about this entire place, it is because no one cares," he said frankly. "But we will see to it that these vents are blocked. Starting tomorrow, we'll also send men in here to clean up this mud and see what else is beneath it. Mayhap even more bodies."

He said it rather grimly, looking at the sea of mud before him. As he and the other men poked around, Annalyla and Maude stood together near the door to the vault, watching anxiously.

"Will you ride into the village and ask the priests if they will give the bones a Christian burial?" Annalyla asked her husband.

Tenner nodded as he stood up and brushed the dirt off his hands. "I will," he said. "You can go with me if you wish. But I have a feeling it will be better if we do not mention where these bones have come from."

Annalyla looked at him curiously. "Why not?"

Tenner looked at her. "Because everyone in Cornwall knows the legend of Baiadepaura," he said. "If we tell the priests we believe this to be the wicked lord of Baiadepaura, I suspect they will refuse to grant the man a Christian burial. We would do better to say we simply found them and leave it at that. In fact, do not tell anyone what you have found here, including that old woman who has been telling you so many tales. She might tell the priests about the bones and then we'd have to find somewhere else to bury them."

Annalyla nodded quickly. "I swear, I'll not tell her anything," she said. Then, she glanced out to the kitchen where Mercy was making bread loaves for the evening meal. "In fact, I have not seen Mawgwen lately. Have you, Maude?"

Maude shook her head. "Come to think of it, I have not."

Annalyla shrugged. "Mayhap she's gone off to tell the men her tales of ghosts and pirates. I think she likes to frighten people with her stories."

That statement caught Tenner's attention. "What about pirates?"

Annalyla moved away from the door, heading in his direction. "I meant to tell you about it when you awoke," she said. "Mawgwen said that pirates have been using Baiadepaura as a base. They sail in a ship called the *Beast of the Seas* and they dock in the cove down below the castle. She said they have been doing this for a few years."

Tenner turned serious very quickly. "Why did you not tell me this before?"

There was concern in in his voice that caused her to feel some apprehension, as if she'd done something wrong. "Because you were sleeping," she said, suddenly hesitant. "Did I do wrong not to wake you with this? I thought it was just another story, since the woman seemed full of them."

Tenner's first reaction was to become upset with her, but he couldn't seem to manage it. It wasn't as if the entire fate of Baiadepaura depended on that information, especially since they already suspected that the castle had been used as a base of some kind. They knew pirates were in the area because they'd seen a ship at sea last night, so Annalyla's information simply confirmed it. He looked at Arlo.

"Then it is as we suspected," he said. "The old woman's story only verifies it. It is a good thing we destroyed the sea path earlier. They will not be able to come up from the cove."

"Did I do wrong not to tell you immediately, Tenner?" Annalyla asked again, anxiety in her voice. "So much has happened this afternoon and it did not seem gravely important, so I apologize if I did not do the right thing."

He could hear the apprehension in her tone. Reaching out, he put an arm around her shoulders. "You did nothing wrong," he said. "It does not truly matter in the end, although if you hear anything like that in the future, please tell me right away. If I am asleep, then wake me. I would rather know sooner and not later."

She nodded, smiling timidly, and he kissed her on the forehead. He smiled in return before turning to the others in the vault.

"Well," he said. "I do not think there is anything more we can do today. Nightfall will be upon us soon, so let us do our rounds and set posts for the night. And I am sure the ladies are well on their way to preparing us a delicious meal."

Thoughts of pirates and old bones were forgotten for the moment as they left the vault and moved into the warm and fragrant kitchen. As Arlo and Graham headed out into the rain, and Maude with them to search for more servants to help with meal preparation in the kitchen, Tenner turned to Annalyla.

"I am very sorry that we had difficulties between us today," he murmured. "I know they were my fault. I shall try to do much better when I'm annoyed or angry."

Annalyla smiled at him, feeling her heart swell with gratitude and warmth. This was her Tenner, the man she'd fallen in love with. Sweet, handsome Tenner who had been kind to her from the start. The man was allowed a little annoyance from time to time. Reaching out, she took his hand.

"And I shall try not to do anything foolish to upset you," she said. "I suppose we must both learn to be patient with one another."

He nodded, bending down to kiss her on the mouth. Her lips were sweet, and warm, and his kiss lingered a moment before he pulled away.

"I will be going about my duties," he said. "If you need me, then send for me."

She nodded, still dwelling on their kiss. "I shall be here overseeing the meal," she said. "Try to stay dry, Ten. We do not need you becoming ill with the damp."

He smirked, looking to the kitchen door and the rain that was coming down in buckets outside. "I shall try," he said. "But no promises. It is chaos out there."

He winked at her as he headed for the door and, with a smile on her lips, Annalyla turned for the stores that were stacked up against the wall to beginning preparing for the evening's meal. But another word from Tenner stopped her.

"I forgot something," he said, leaning against the doorjamb as the rain poured down behind him. "Maude told me something and I want to know if it is true."

Annalyla looked at him curiously. "What did she tell you?"

"That you adore me."

Annalyla flushed a bright shade of red, averting her gaze because she was so embarrassed at being caught in a truth of her own making. Of course, she adored him, but she wasn't so shameless that she would tell him without restraint. Struggling not to look foolish, she turned back to the barrels.

"What do you think, de Velt?" she asked. "You have proven yourself kind and humorous. And you are very handsome. I would be a fool if I did not adore some part of you."

"Why not adore all of me?"

"And you also have an ungainly amount of conceit."

He laughed, going to her as she worked over a barrel with her back to him. He grabbed her from behind, pulling her against him and nuzzling her neck.

"I adore you, too," he whispered. "Never forget it."

After kissing her ear, he was gone, disappearing out into the ungodly rain. Annalyla stood there a moment, her hand on her neck where he had kissed her, with a giddy smile on her face.

All was right in the world again.

With renewed vigor, she went back to work.

CHAPTER SEVENTEEN

WHEN DARKNESS CAME, they moved.

The *Beast of the Seas* was anchored out to sea, just off the coast, because the seas were so rough and there were rocks closer to the shore that could tear up the hull. Therefore, Raleigh dropped anchor in Crackington Bay, south of Baiadepaura by a few miles, and took two small skiffs in to the beach just as darkness fell.

It was a difficult beaching of the skiffs because of the tide and the crashing waves, but they managed to pull the fragile little boats onto the sandy shore, one of the only soft sand coves on the entire west coast of Cornwall. They pulled the boats up far enough so that they couldn't be swept out by waves or a rising tide. Once they were secured, the men gathered their weapons and took the narrow path up the cliff.

The trek to Baiadepaura wasn't a long one in the least – only four miles to the north – but a storm had blown in from the west and it had been lashing the land for several hours. As the sun set, it only grew worse, so they'd had to fight the wind and rain all the way up the coast, walking a fisherman's path through heavy sea grass and scrub.

Their mission was clear.

There were twenty-one of them, the majority of Raleigh's crew, but as he put it, twenty-one of his men were worth fifty of a land army. His men were scrappers, born and bred to fight and kill by any means necessary. That was why he was confident that they would win whatever battle they faced. While the English soldiers were gathering their wits and trying to fight a clean and honorable battle, Raleigh and Alastair and the rest of his men would be fighting dirty. At a distinct disadvantage with fewer men than the English probably carried, they would win any way they could.

With them, they mostly had daggers – and many of them. Daggers to fight with, daggers to throw. They weren't archers, nor did they carry arrows, which swelled with the moist sea air and weren't accurate from a moving vessel, so they'd become adept with an assortment of daggers. Raleigh carried a nasty one, about a foot and a half in length, with a serrated edge on one side. It was a horrific weapon that had killed a good many men and this night it would claim a few more, God willing.

Aye, Raleigh prayed for such things.

He prayed for victory.

The weather was working in their favor. Storms concealed their movements and they'd learned to love them. The path cut inland for a time and they struggled through the mud and wind but, soon enough, they were in view of the sea again, which was faintly illuminated on this night. The moon behind the clouds was full, giving the clouds a glow all their own, which reflected to the rough seas below. As they pushed on in a single file line, hidden by the tall grass, Alastair caught up to Raleigh.

"Do ye think old Mawgwen was able tae get rid of the *Sassenach*?" he asked, wiping water from his face.

Raleigh's focus was up ahead. "We shall know soon enough," he said. Then, he came to a halt, waiting until the rest of his men caught up so he could speak to them in a group. He waved his hands at them, bringing the group in close. "Come near, lads. 'Tis time tae speak of what will come."

When the men ganged up around him, Raleigh pulled out a damp kerchief and wiped the water from his eyes.

"'Tis time tae take back our castle," he said. "The old witch from the tavern was tae convince them tae leave, but if she dinna, we'll realize it soon enough. If they've left, then we'll not need our weapons. But if they're still there..."

"Then we kill them!" one of the men spat, holding up his wicked-looking dagger. "I've a hunger tae draw *Sassenach* blood this night!"

The others grumbled in agreement, a motley mass of men who stank of salt and the sea. They were out of place on land, and they looked like it – like creatures that had just crawled up out of the deep. With water rolling down their faces and the wind whipping through wet clothing, they were beasts looking for a kill.

And Raleigh knew it.

"Listen tae me, lads," he said. "We may not have another chance like this. We'll approach from the south and Alastair will take half of ye tae the mouth of the sea path. The wall that was there is damaged and it will make an easy breach. I'll take the rest of ye behind the keep, on the path that goes along the cliff's edge, and we'll come up near the old kitchen. Do ye know where I mean?"

Heads were bobbing in agreement. As lightning lit up the sky overhead and thunder rolled, Raleigh glanced up to beseech the weather gods.

"Keep the storm, just for a little while longer," he said to the sky before returning his focus to his men. "If the *Sassenach* have abandoned the castle for the sake of old Mawgwen, then 'tis all well and good. But if they haven't, then we go tae the keep first. My guess is that the soft *Sassenach* commanders will be there, and we'll slit their throats in their beds. Cut off their heads and display them tae their men, and, surely, they'll run. Everyone knows the *Sassenach* canna fight without their knights in command. Cut off the head and we shall know victory!"

His men were eager, cheering at the thought of carving English flesh that night. More thunder and lightning crashed overhead, and Raleigh waved his arm at his men, moving them on towards their destination of Baiadepaura. Fighting through a new wave of vicious rain, they came up to the crest of a hill only to see Baiadepaura Castle on the next hill, across the cliffs, like a beacon against the stormy night.

One glance was all they needed to see that there were lights everywhere in the castle – in the keep, against the windows, and on the walls. That told them what they needed to know, that old Mawgwen had been unsuccessful in chasing the English away.

They knew what they had to do.

Crouching low to stay in line with the tops of the sea grass, they began to move swiftly across the path, knowing that the rain and darkness were keeping their movements concealed.

As they drew closer to the structure, they split into their two groups, with Alastair taking his men towards the sea path and Raleigh taking his to the path that led along the cliffs behind the keep.

Had the walls been in full repair, they would have never been able to even make it to the sea path, but the fact that the English hadn't had time to fix any of the walls yet gave them the advantage they needed.

They were going to take back what belonged to them.

The Bay of Fear would take on new meaning this night.

CHAPTER EIGHTEEN

THE HALL WAS a place of warmth and laughter this night.

It was true that the weather was horrific outside. But inside the old building with the leaking roof, everything was warm and smoky, with men gambling and a few of them even singing, drunk on the barrels of wine that the quartermaster had brought from Seven Crosses. Perhaps to Tenner and Arlo and Graham, it was any normal night, but to Annalyla, it was a special night.

It was the first night she felt as if she were truly home.

Tenner and Arlo were laughing over some adventure they'd had in Exeter, something about an old acquaintance who was more an enemy than a friend, challenging one or both of them when he was drunk. It seemed that Arlo distracted the man while Tenner stole his purse, especially after the man had referred to Tenner as a "devil-eyed beast." When the man finally sobered up and went looking for his money, Tenner and Arlo told him that a whore had stolen it, leading him to raid a brothel at the end of town where the working women had beaten him severely.

It was all quite humorous to them. Even Graham was smiling. Tenner and Arlo had admitted Graham into their small brotherhood and made him feel welcome, which was a camaraderie that Graham hadn't felt in a very long time. Spending his time at Roseden as he had, with only Cain St. Lo as his single male companion, he was much more comfortable and in his element with a pair of knights.

Life, for Graham, was starting to shine again.

In fact, it was shining for them all, and routines were already being established. Nearly all of the men were crowded into the hall this night because the weather was so bad, and with only seven women to tend to so many men, Annalyla and Maude were moving around the hall, making sure everything was attended to and that the men had enough to eat. Old Mawgwen had yet to be found, so Annalyla and Mercy, and a couple of the other women, had prepared the meal with the help of the old quartermaster, but it was an excellent meal to be had.

The salted beef had been soaked and boiled, producing a broth of sorts that a stew had been made from. Annalyla had cut up onions and carrots and turnips, all of it boiled with the meat and, by suppertime, it was a hearty meal. Coupled with the bread that Mercy had baked, they had quite a feast on this stormy night.

Hearing the laughter and the lively conversation was like music to Annalyla's ears. It had been like this at Netherghyll when she'd fostered those years ago and she'd loved the energy of it. But the years she'd spent at Roseden afterwards were like living in a tomb. No laughter, only a strict sense of austerity and schemes to land rich husbands.

Thoughts of Mother Angel had crossed her mind since her marriage to Tenner, but only briefly. She honestly didn't think about the woman other than to be grateful she hadn't come to Baiadepaura. Sometimes she thought of Ivor, that strange earl who seemed far too solicitous to her, and she also thought of Lady Jane and the night the woman had tried to break into her room, perhaps searching for her lost love.

In that respect, Lady Jane wasn't unlike the ghost of the last lord of Baiadepaura, wandering the halls in the search for his wife's amulet. Both Jane and Faustus had tragic love stories, and as Annalyla turned to look at Tenner as the man chatted animatedly with Arlo, she could only feel deep gratitude that her love story hadn't turned out tragic as well. She'd been vastly fortunate to find her happy ending.

"Annie," Maude said as she came up beside her, handing her an empty pewter pitcher. "It is your turn to fill this with the last of the stew. I went the last two times."

Annalyla giggled. "Why me?" she demanded lightly. "I am the chatelaine. I should not have to fetch stew."

Maude pointed to the north end of the hall where four of the servant women seemed to be cleaning up something from the floor.

"Then you can go over there and finish cleaning up the vomit," she said. "They had a drinking game going on over there and more than one man could not hold his wine. One became sick and then several others followed. Well? Shall I tell the servants that you shall clean it up and they can go to the kitchens?"

Annalyla rolled her eyes. "God, no," she hissed, snatching the pitcher. "I will go to the kitchens. I would rather get wet than mop up the contents of someone's stomach."

Maude snorted at her, following her all the way to the door of the great hall where the storm was raging beyond. Annalyla paused at the door, frowning at the nasty weather, as Maude came up behind her and gave her a little shove, right out into the rain. It was in good humor, and Annalyla shook a fist at her in response.

But she couldn't keep from laughing as she did it.

As Maude laughed, Annalyla began running across the cobbled bailey, which was slippery with the rain. In fact, she almost slipped twice, using the heavy pewter pitcher as ballast so she wouldn't lose her balance. Skipping closer to the stairs that led down to the kitchen, she had her head lowered to keep the rain from her eyes, but also so she could see where she was going. Just as she neared the steps, someone coming up the stairs reached out and grabbed her.

Startled, Annalyla looked up into the face of a man she didn't recognize. In fact, he wasn't dressed like a soldier; he was in leather and wool, smelling of rot and the sea, and the leather cap on his head was worn and tattered. When he smiled at her, a most wicked smile, she could see that he was missing most of his teeth.

Instinctively, she tried to pull away, but he held tight. Then, she saw several other men coming up behind them, all of them with daggers in their hands. It took Annalyla a moment to realize that this was a group of invaders, men who meant to do them all great harm, and in a panic, she swung the pewter pitcher, braining the man who held her on the side of his skull. He released her and staggered back, falling back on the steps and crashing into some of the men behind him. That action gave Annalyla the moment she needed to break away and scream.

"Maude!" she screamed. "*Raiders!*"

She could see Maude still at the door of the hall, but she didn't know if the woman had heard her. She started to run, but the ground was so slippery she ended up nearly falling as she struggled to gain traction. In her periphery, she could see another man making a swipe at her, and she screamed again, picking up her skirts and running as fast as she could across the slick stones.

Annalyla knew she had no chance of making it to the hall before someone grabbed her, so her best option was to run into the keep and find a place to hide until Tenner could come for her. Behind her, she could hear cursing and yelling, and more men suddenly burst forth at the southern end of the bailey, their blades flashing in the light that was emitting from the hall.

It was a full-scale invasion from the sea as Annalyla headed for the keep, praying she could stay out of sight until Tenner could help her. In truth, there was nowhere else she could run to, so the great doors of the keep beckoned and she headed towards them, praying she could reach them – and safety – in time.

Praying that Tenner would be able to help her before it was too late.

"BREACH!" MAUDE SCREAMED.

The woman had lived in castles long enough to know the protocol of an attack, and the moment she saw men with weapons bursting forth from the seaward side of the complex and grabbing at Annalyla, she started to scream.

The great hall quieted down in an instant.

"Breach!" she screamed again, turning towards the table where her husband and Tenner and Graham were. "Tenner, Annie is in trouble! The keep! *Go to the keep!*"

Somewhat inebriated with all of the wine he'd had that evening, Tenner's head was swimming a little, but it did nothing to dampen his response. He went from laughing and joking into immediate command and control mode as he hurdled over the table with Arlo and Graham right behind him.

In fact, the entire hall was scrambling, men rushing for the doors, and Tenner was at the head of it. He reached the door in time to see Annalyla disappearing into the keep with a man in pursuit. And as he stepped out into the driving rain, he could see many figures emerging from the darkness, with weapons in hand.

He couldn't tell how many men there were, but that didn't matter. They'd been caught off-guard and he felt like a fool. A stupid, useless fool. But his feelings aside, all that mattered to him was getting to his wife, who was running for her life. Unfortunately, he didn't have his broadsword; it was in the keep where he'd left it. But he did have a dagger on his body, a rather large one, and as he unsheathed it, he turned to Maude, who was still standing by the door.

"Stay here!" he barked. "Find a place to hide and stay there. Do you understand me?"

Maude was terrified; he could see it in her eyes, but she nodded quickly. As Arlo rushed to his wife to help her hide, Tenner and the rest of the men charged from the hall.

It was a stream of men, most of whom were drunk or on their way to being drunk, confronting a gang of men who were well-prepared and sober. That gave the invaders the advantage, even over several times their number in manpower, at least for the moment. The sounds of weapons clashing could be heard as the two groups came together, the noise of battle now mixing with the howling storm. With the clash of fighting all around him, Tenner ran straight for the keep.

But it wasn't a clear path.

Immediately, he was confronted by a man with a massive dagger, arched in shape like a scimitar. Tenner's dagger was considerably smaller and, very quickly, he was in hand-to-hand combat with a man who was seriously trying to kill him.

It was a battle for his life.

Tenner was feeling so very stupid. He'd let his guard down and he shouldn't have. Worse still, his men had followed his example and they'd let their guards down, too. Their second night at the derelict old castle, and no one had been expecting an attack from the seaward side. The portcullises were secured, the sea path destroyed, but there were still gaping holes in their security which the men on the walls had failed to protect.

As the storm lashed them, Tenner had no time for foolery, fighting with a man who was clearly not his equal. But he took a bad step on the slippery stones and he felt something crack in his ankle. Slipping, he went down heavily on his left side, all the while defending himself from the onslaught of the attacker as pain shot up his left leg.

Instantly, he knew he was in a bad way.

But he didn't give up. He had de Velt and de Lohr blood in him, and surrender was not an option. As the attacker came closer and lifted his arm to deliver a powerful blow, Tenner took advantage and rammed his dagger into the man's underarm. As his opponent crumpled in a heap, Tenner leaped to his feet.

Unfortunately, he'd done damage to his ankle, so walking was extremely painful and difficult, made worse by the slippery stones. All around him there was fighting going on, but he paid no attention to it. His only focus was on getting to the keep where his wife was struggling for her life. He could feel a blind panic welling up within him, a desperation and fear he'd never felt before. The idea of Annalyla at the mercy of a marauder put terror in his heart the likes of which he'd never experienced.

He had to get to her.

Limping and hopping on his good leg, he moved faster than he ever thought he could, given his injury, and made his way towards the dark and uninviting keep.

I'm coming, Annie!

ONCE ANNALYLA HAD run into the keep, her terror had taken her in a direction she shouldn't have gone. While there were heavy doors on the master's chambers in the south side of the keep, she'd mistakenly rushed to her right once she entered the keep, which only took her to the damaged northern wing.

Unfortunately, her attacker was right behind her and she couldn't turn and go the opposite direction. She would have run right into him. So, much like a chicken with its head cut off, she ran indiscriminately, anywhere she thought there might be safety, and she ended up racing up the old flight of stones steps that led to the north wing, the one that was so badly damaged. Up the stairs she went, hearing her pursuer right behind her, grunting and cursing because he was having to run after his unwilling quarry.

Annalyla struggled to rein in her panic because if she couldn't think clearly, then she was as good as dead. But now, she was on the second floor of the northern wing and there were only two chambers here, from what she remembered. Oddly enough, they both had sturdy doors, so she ran into the first chamber and slammed the panel, struggling to close it as the attacker came up behind her and threw his weight on the door.

Annalyla knew in an instant that she would have no chance of keeping him out. Already, he was pushing the door in, grabbing for her. He managed to grab hold of her sleeve, by the shoulder, and in a panic, she bit him. It had the desired effect; he swiftly released her, and she threw herself on the door, catching his wrist. He growled in pain and, angered, gave a good shove, nearly opening the door completely.

Annalyla suddenly moved away from the door and the man fell into the room, literally. As he was wallowing on his face, she leaped over him and ran straight into the other chamber, the one missing part of the roof and with part of one wall missing, all the way down to the floor.

Annalyla thought briefly of taking the stairs and running out of the keep, but she thought it would be safer to lock herself in somewhere, even if it was a partially collapsed room. It would be a heavy door between her and the attackers, so she ran into the room and slammed the door, only to discover there was no bolt on it. Before she could open the door and run again, her attacker was there, again throwing himself against the panel.

The blow sent Annalyla stumbling across the room, over near the corner where the wall was missing and it was a three-story drop to the ground below. When she finally caught her balance and looked up, her attacker was standing in the open door, looking at her.

But he wasn't charging her. Oddly enough, he was just standing there, looking at her, probably because he knew she was cornered now. She couldn't get away. Annalyla backed away, her eyes never leaving him.

"Get out of here," she hissed. "Leave me alone!"

The man smiled and rubbed the left side of his head. It was the same man she'd smacked with the heavy pitcher and he was fingering a lump on his scalp.

"Ye gave a good fight, missy," he said. "I congratulate ye."

He was starting to move towards her, slowly and deliberately, and Annalyla's heart pounded painfully with fear.

"I told you to go away," she said, mustering a threat. "My husband will be here any moment and he will kill you."

The man shook his head. "More than likely, he's already dead," he said. "Did ye not see my men in the bailey? They'll kill every man here.

There is no chance for anyone."

Annalyla had seen some men with him, initially, but she had no idea how many there were. The way he was talking, there was evidently a massive army in the bailey now, killing everything that wasn't part of them. The mere idea was terrifying. But she held her ground, refusing to give in to the fear that was clawing at her.

She had to fight!

"What kind of men do you think are here?" she asked in a condescending tone. "There are seasoned knights protecting this place. Do you truly think your men can kill them?"

He cocked his head. "I do."

He seemed arrogant, but not in a boastful way. In a factual way. He believed every word he said and for every step he took towards her, Annalyla took a step back.

He was stalking her.

"Who *are* you?" she hissed. "What do you want?"

He smiled lazily. "We want our castle back."

We want our castle back. She eyed him rather curiously. "Back?" she repeated. "But this castle does not belong to you. It belongs to the Earl of Tiverton."

He shook his head. "It belongs tae *me*," he said firmly. "Tiverton, is it? Did the Earl of Cornwall sell it tae him?"

She continued to view him with great confusion as well as fear. "Nay," she said. "The king gave it to him, I believe. What do you mean it belongs to you? *Who are you?*"

It was the second time she'd asked the question and, this time, he answered. "My name isna important," he said. "But my men and me, we own the seas. We take what we want, and we want Baiadepaura. 'Tis a place no one will have, but I will. And I want it back."

Annalyla stared at him a moment before her eyes widened. "Pirates!" she suddenly spat. "You're the pirate who has been living here!"

He seemed amused. "So ye know that, do ye?"

"I was told. Is it true?"

"'Tis."

Annalyla could hardly believe she was facing off against a pirate. She'd never imagined she'd ever even see one much less be cornered by one, and the fear she felt was magnified. She remembered old Mawgwen speaking of the pirates and she further remembered the old woman trying to discourage her from staying at Baiadepaura by telling her of the legends and curses. Perhaps, this pirate knew nothing of them. In a desperate move, she thought that if she told the man the terrible things of the castle, he would no longer want it. Maybe he'd go away and leave them alone. Having no weapon to fend the man off with, she used the only weapon she had –

Fear.

"Why would you want a place like this?" she asked. "The place his haunted, you know. A wicked lord lived here and his angry ghost still roams the grounds. Would you really want such a place?"

The man began to resume his slow advance on her; for every step he took forward, she took a step back.

"I know," he said casually. "I've seen the ghost. We've all seen the ghost."

Annalyla could see that her words hadn't stopped him. They hadn't even slowed him down. She was beginning to feel rain and she nervously glanced behind her only to see that the broken wall and the drop to the ground below were looming ever closer. She couldn't go too much further without stopping unless she wanted to fall to her death. Panic began to overtake her again, but a strong sense of survival filled her veins.

"Do you know what the ghost is looking for?" she asked, chattering in an increasingly terrified tone. "An amulet. Something that belonged to his wife. That's the legend – he and his wife were wrongly killed by villagers for a crime they did not commit. He roams this place looking for something he gave his wife."

That didn't slow the advance of the pirate. "We've seen him," he said again. "He comes with the wind. But 'tis not enough tae keep me away, missy. I need Baiadepaura. Everyone knows the legend, so it keeps men away, and for what I must do, I dunna need men trying tae invade my privacy. Ye should have left when ye were given the chance."

Annalyla blinked. "Given… given the chance?"

"When the old woman told ye tae leave."

Her eyes widened. "Mawgwen!" she gasped. Suddenly, the old woman's presence became clear and all of the things the woman had said made a great deal of sense. Of course she'd been trying to force them to leave; she'd been in league with the pirates! "*You* sent her here?"

The man nodded. "It 'twould be easier if ye chose tae leave on yer own," he said. "But ye dinna."

Annalyla felt more rain than ever, pelting her head and back, and she turned to see that she was at the end of her movement. She could go no further. Horror and tremendous sadness filled her, knowing that there was nothing more she could do. The pirate would soon be upon her and unless she wanted to jump, her only option was to fight him off.

Or die trying.

God help me.

"I am sorry that your castle has been taken away," she said, her voice trembling. "But it never belonged to you. Mayhap, it truly belongs to no one but the ghost who roams the halls, but killing me won't solve anything. It will not make this castle any more yours. If anything, it will bring more trouble upon you."

That brought him to a halt. "Who says I'm going tae kill ye?" he said, his gaze drifting over her in a lewd manner. "I'm going tae take ye tae my ship and ye can warm my bed. Ye're too fine tae kill, lady, as long as ye please me. And ye *will* please me."

Bile rose in Annalyla's throat. "I would rather be dead."

He lifted a dark eyebrow. "That can be arranged, missy."

He took a step in her direction but commotion at the door caught his attention. He turned to see a very large man in the doorway with a large dagger in his hand.

And hell followed with him.

TENNER HAD ARRIVED.

The first thing he saw was Annalyla backed up against the ledge of the broken wall and terror filled him. Swollen ankle and all, he wasn't going to let that stop him. But the unfortunate fact was that the pirate was closer to Annalyla than he was, and the man reached out to grab her. In Annalyla's struggle to avoid being captured, she knocked herself off-balance and ended up clutching at the broken wall to keep from falling over the edge and into the dark abyss below.

It was Tenner's worst nightmare. He limped across the floor, moving as quickly as he could, but the pirate made another swipe at Annalyla and she screamed. Tenner was certain he was either going to watch his wife being shoved to her death, or watch her bleed to death when her throat was slit by the pirate with a very large dagger. All he could see in the dim light was struggling, and a man threatening his wife, but his bad ankle was preventing him from moving any faster. When he was halfway across the chamber, water on the floor made him slip and he ended up crashing onto one knee. But he was up again, wielding his dagger, in time to see something that would change his life forever.

Something came between the pirate and Annalyla.

A mist.

Even with the driving rain coming through the broken roof, a mist was forming, taking on a faint shape. *A man.* Tenner hadn't even realized he'd come to a halt, shocked to the bone as the mist enveloped the pirate and the man abruptly stumbled back. In fact, the pirate began to shriek and weep, waving his hands around as if trying to shove the mist away, but the mist only grew more dense.

An icy wind began to whip around the room, like a vortex, and

Annalyla's hair was whipped into a frenzy. She'd managed to recapture her balance, now leaning heavily against the broken wall as the pirate was driven back by the invading mist, pushed towards the edge of the broken wall with the three-story drop to the hard earth below.

Step by step, inch by inch, the pirate moved away from the mist, backwards, trying to fight it off, screaming that he was being choked. As Annalyla and Tenner watched in astonishment, the pirate took a misstep and plunged over the ledge.

Annalyla saw the man land on his head, and then he moved no more.

It was the most terrifying and shocking thing she'd ever seen but, suddenly, Tenner was beside her, his arms going around her as he pulled her away from the broken wall. Annalyla threw her arms around his neck, clinging to him as she realized she was finally safe.

It was over.

"Are you well?" Tenner asked, his voice trembling. "Did he hurt you?"

Annalyla shook her head. "Nay," she said, pulling her face from the crook of his neck. "He did not hurt me. Are *you* well?"

He nodded, a sigh of relief escaping his lips. "I am well," he said, ignoring his throbbing ankle. "All that matters to me is that you are unscathed. I…"

He abruptly trailed off as he caught sight of the mist over Annalyla's shoulder and they both turned to see that the eerie form had not dissipated. It was still there, still lingering. As Tenner simply stood there, his uncertainty at what he was seeing overwhelming him, Annalyla knew exactly what she was seeing because she'd seen it before, earlier in the day. There was no fear, no terror in her heart.

She knew.

"Thank you," she said to the mist. "You saved my life."

The mist seemed to take on a more solid form and the shape of a man became more defined. The storm outside was easing somewhat, though it was still raining, and the clouds began to move enough so that the white moonlight was beginning to beam through.

Even more clearly now, they could see a man.

Annalyla couldn't take her eyes off of him. She felt an overwhelming need to speak to the ghost because, for certain, this had been a day of discovery. She wondered if the ghost already knew what she had discovered. Was that why he had saved her life? Because he knew how hard she'd worked to find what he'd been looking for?

"I know what happened to you," she said. "I read the hide that you left behind. You begged for mercy from the villagers who thought you brought a sickness upon them, but they killed you anyway. I do not know all of it, but I know now that there is some truth to the legend. The truth is that there was a sickness, and it is true that you were murdered because of it. But it also true that you are not wicked. I am very sorry the villagers killed you and your Anyu. You were greatly wronged. But I think I have something that you are looking for."

Gently, she pulled away from Tenner, who was reluctant to let her go. Digging into the pocket of her skirt, she pulled forth the twisted gold amulet, the horsehead that was barely discernable. She extended it to the ghost.

"I truly do not know if this is something you want, or if it was merely a legend, but I found what I believe is the horsehead amulet you gave to your wife," she said, holding the small piece up so that it glistened in the cold moonlight. "I was digging in the vault and I found it. I also found you. Or, at least, I believe it is you. My husband and I are going to ask the priests to give you a proper burial and I shall make sure this amulet is buried with you. I hope that makes you happy. I am so very sorry that you were wrongly killed, but I assure you, I will make sure you and this amulet are properly buried. Mayhap you and Anyu will finally find peace because of it."

The ghost simply stood there, undulating in the moonlight, before moving in her direction. Behind her, she could feel Tenner stiffen.

"Annie…"

She could hear the hazard in his voice, fearful that the ghost that had just killed the pirate was now coming towards her. But she held up a hand to him, quieting him, and remained in place, unmoving as the ghost approached. The closer it came, the more defined it became, and they could see the distinct shape of a large man, a big head, and then a hand emerging from the mist. It reached out, touching the amulet as Annalyla held it aloft. A voice came again, like a whispered breath, and it blew past her ear.

Gratias.

And with that, it was gone, vanished as if it had never been there. Now, all that remained was the wind and the gentle rain, and moonbeams streaming down from the clouds. Annalyla and Tenner stood there a moment, unmoving and unspeaking, until Tenner finally broke the silence.

"Annie?"

"Aye?

"I… I heard it, too."

Annalyla turned to look at him with tears in her eyes. "Did you truly?"

Tenner was pale, his eyes still wide with shock. "I did," he said as if he couldn't believe it. "I heard *Gratias.* He thanked you."

Annalyla nodded and tears fell from her eyes. "I told you that I had seen him today, and that he'd spoken to me," she whispered. "I did not lie."

Reaching out, he pulled her against him, holding her tightly, never more grateful for anything in his life. As she sobbed softly, he kissed the top of her head, thinking on what he'd just witnessed.

He knew exactly what he'd seen.

So much for the logical man.

"He saved you," he said, incredulity in his tone. "That… that ghost, that *thing*, saved your life. Had it not intervened, God only knows what would have happened. You were right all along, Annie. The Devil of Baiadepaura is not a devil, after all. In that one act of salvation, he destroyed two hundred years of rumor and legend."

"But how will people know?" she wept.

"They will know because I am going to tell them. And if they think I'm mad… I do not care. I truly do not."

Annalyla held him tighter. That was all the response he needed. Tenner always said he had to see to believe and, tonight, he'd seen. And he believed.

The Devil of Baiadepaura was real. And it was a devil no more.

That night, the men of the *Beast of the Seas* met with a far more skilled and better-armed English army, and within an hour of attacking Baiadepaura Castle, all but two of them were dead, including Raleigh and Alastair. The women were safe and the castle secure when, just before dawn, Tenner and Arlo, and twenty men dressed in some of the clothing they'd stolen from the pirates, return to Crackington Cove and took the skiffs out to the *Beast of the Seas*, moored out to sea and awaiting the return of her victorious crew.

But there was no victory to be had.

It took Tenner and his men all of ten minutes to secure the ship and wrangle the skeleton crew, and the ship itself was sailed up the coast only to dock below Baiadepaura on the dawn of a new, clear day. As the sun burst over the horizon and illuminated the wet and weary land, the ship was now a new possession of Tenner de Velt. The *Beast of the Seas* would eventually be re-christened *The Devil of Baiadepaura* and used to escort merchant ships along the Cornwall coast.

There was no more fearsome or proud sight.

But there was more. As promised, two days after the pirate attack on Baiadepaura, Tenner, Arlo, and Graham gathered all of the bone remnants they could find in the vault and put them into a chest along with the remains of the horsehead amulet. Since legend said that Faustus and Anyu were both burned, they could only assume that some of the bone fragments were Anyu's, and Tenner and Annalyla, along with a small escort of soldiers, headed north into Bude, to the Church of St. Peter. There, they paid the priests handsomely to give the bones a Christian burial. In the years to come, they would return to the grave to pay their respects to Faustus de Paura and to thank him for his otherworldly role in saving Annalyla's life.

As Tenner would say repeatedly, had he not seen it with his own eyes, he would have never believed it.

The skeptic was finally a believer.

Baiadepaura Castle was a peaceful place after that dark and stormy night. No more ghosts, no more unholy winds or howls. Faustus and Anyu had found peace, the conclusion to an ending that had been two hundred years in the making. It wasn't exactly a happy ending for the pair, but they were together in the end and that was all that mattered. The castle became a serene place, and once fully rebuilt and restored, became the envy of every fighting man from Penzance to Cardiff, a magnificent garrison ruled by the fair but iron fist of Sir Tenner de Velt.

It was the stuff of legends.

Baiadepaura Castle became everything Tenner and Annalyla had ever hoped it would be, and legends of ghosts and curses soon faded from the vernacular of Cornwall. Baiadepaura was no longer called the Bay of Fear as it had been for so long. A new generation saw the hope and strength of the fortress, rebuilt by a de Velt, no less, and it soon took its place among the great and respectable castles of Cornwall, with a benevolent lord and lady to rule over it.

The Bay of Fear was no more.

EPILOGUE

One year later

IT WAS A gentle rain that fell along the Cornwall coast, not one of the tempests that were so common to the area. This rain was more of a mist, wetting man and beast alike, but the men of Baiadepaura Castle moved through it as if it weren't there. It misted so frequently that it was simply part of their daily lives. On this day, however, there was a great deal of activity in the bailey as the big portcullis began to crank open. Chains creaked as the gate slowly lifted to the approaching party.

It was a contingent from Seven Crosses, escorted by Tenner and Arlo. They'd gone all the way to Tiverton to collect precious cargo, which was now returning to Baiadepaura. Annalyla stood in the windows of her husband's comfortable solar, watching the gate and knowing that, finally, the prize had arrived.

"My lady?"

Annalyla turned to the entry to the solar, seeing a knight standing there. He was new to Baiadepaura, having come all the way from Canterbury Castle last month. Sir Beaufort de Fira was young, with a crown of curly blonde hair and bright blue eyes that lit up his entire face. He as a handsome man and very kind, and Annalyla saw very quickly why Tenner thought so highly of the man. He was the consummate knight, talented and honorable. After ten months of command at Baiadepaura, Tenner had sent for his friend to come and serve with him.

Beau arrived as swiftly as if he'd traveled on angel's wings.

"Come in," she said pleasantly, beckoning the man. "They are just arriving now."

Beau entered the solar, his focus on the scene out in the bailey as a large escort, including a fortified carriage, entered the grounds.

"My God," he breathed. "She's really here. Tenner did it."

Annalyla smiled at him. "Did you truly have any doubt?"

Beau shrugged. "Nay," he said truthfully. "Not really. I know that Ten can be convincing when he wants to be, but…"

Annalyla finished for him. "But the earl is protective over Lady Jane and you had your doubts that he would permit her to come and visit," she said. When he nodded, she laughed softly. "Never fear, Beau. Once Tenner de Velt sets his mind on something, it is as good as done. In this case, he wanted to bring Lady Jane to you since her father banished you from Seven Crosses. He has spoken of it to me before, many times. He said what happened between you was a true tragedy."

Beau nodded, though his attention was riveted to the carriage that was now coming to a halt. "I kept telling myself that what happened was God's will," he said. "Everything that happened, it was simply meant to happen that way. But the truth was that I was resentful. And I was miserable."

Annalyla looked at the young knight for a moment, seeing the utter hope and delight on his face. It was so very sweet to see, a love story that would, perhaps, know an ending other than the one Ivor had condemned them to. Turning away from the window, she rubbed at her enormously swollen belly as she headed over to the nearest chair, settling herself down upon it.

Heavy with child, Tenner had forbidden his wife from traveling to Seven Crosses to retrieve Lady Jane FitzJohn. Arlo and Maude had gone instead, as Maude had known Lady Jane before her accident. Annalyla understood, of course, but she'd missed him terribly in the five days that he'd been gone. A very short separation, but when one was in love, any amount of separation seemed like an eternity.

She could see that very same sentiment on Beau's face.

His separation from Jane had been an eternity.

"Beau," she said hesitantly. "You know… you *are* aware that Lady Jane is not the woman you once knew, don't you? What I mean to say is… I know you are excited to see her, but I am told the injury changed her dramatically."

Beau nodded. "I know, my lady," he said, turning to look at her. His blue eyes were twinkling. "I think you have been fearful to say anything to me since Tenner came up with the plot to bring Jane to Baiadepaura. But the truth is that I know she has changed. I was able to see her briefly after her injury and, in the time I spent with her, it was true that she had changed a great deal. But I could still see the Jane I fell in love with in her eyes. She is still there, underneath everything."

"You truly believe that?"

"I do."

Annalyla smiled at the man. Love, truly, was blind. "Then I pray you come to know her again while she is here," she said. "I wish you all of the happiness in the world, Beau."

He went to her, then, taking a knee beside her and taking her hand, kissing it gallantly. "Tenner is a very fortunate man," he said. "I have known him for years and he has always been a man of character and strength. There are times I have seen compassion in him, but this sentiment that he seems to hide… I saw it briefly when Jane was injured. It seems to me that you have brought out that side of him. He is no longer afraid to show it. I shall ever be grateful to you for how happy you have made him."

Annalyla was touched by his tribute. "As he has made me happy, too," she said. "Maude once said that Tenner was a secret romantic, and I believe that. He very much wants to see his friends as happy as he is."

Beau started to reply when noise from the entry caught his attention. Quickly, he stood up, turning to the door just in time to see Tenner entering. The man was in full mail and protection, looking like a powerful battle lord, but the expression on his face was exceedingly soft as he went to his wife. Annalyla stood up about the time he reached her and he stretched out, putting his arms around her, gently.

"Greetings, sweetling," he said sweetly, kissing her soft mouth. "You are looking well and beautiful."

Annalyla hugged him tightly. "I am very well," she said. "How was your journey?"

Tenner kissed her again, on the lips and on the cheek. "Uneventful," he said. He looked at Beau as if just noticing the man. "Well? Has all been quiet since I've been away?"

Beau nodded, but he was distracted, hearing more commotion in the entry. "Aye," he said. "Very quiet, except we caught some children trying to steal one of our cows yesterday. Young boys, in fact."

Tenner frowned. "Are they hungry?" he asked. "Did you seek their parents to see if they are in need of food?"

Beau lifted his eyebrows. "Their parents were not destitute," he said. "In fact, one of the fathers was so outraged that he let me beat his son with a switch before he took a turn himself. I am sure that will be the last time that lad tries anything so foolish. One does not steal cows from the great Lord of Baiadepaura's herd simply for the thrill of it."

Tenner snorted. "Boys stealing cows," he said. "If that is the least they do, then that is hardly a beating offense. As a child, I did things that were much worse."

Annalyla looked at him. "Like what?"

"I could tell you, but you would probably leave me and never return," he said. "Therefore, in the interest of our marriage, I refuse to answer."

As she started to giggle at him, more people began entering the solar. Annalyla, Tenner, and Beau turned to see Arlo entering the room, followed by Maude leading a young woman with her. Maude had her arm around the woman's shoulders and was speaking softly and steadily to her. Beau's gentle expression told Annalyla everything she needed to know about the new arrival.

Lady Jane FitzJohn had arrived.

Annalyla took a good look at the woman. In truth, she'd never actually seen her. Even on that night last year at Seven Crosses when the woman had tried to break into her chamber, Annalyla had never taken a good look at her.

Now, she was.

Lady Jane was fair, with pale blonde hair pulled into a braid and big, blue eyes. She had an angelic beauty, rather delicate, which was surprising, considering the force with which the woman howled.

But she also looked a little confused, and even a little scared, as Maude led her into the chamber. Beau, unable to stay away, timidly approached.

"Jane?" he said softly. "Janie, 'tis me. 'Tis Beau."

Jane's wide-eyed gaze turned to him and, for a moment, no one breathed. No one spoke. They were all waiting to see her reaction to her former lover, a man that she had cried for constantly since the day he'd been exiled. But she didn't react at first – she simply looked at him with a gaze that showed nothing at all in her expression. No recognition, no joy.

Undeterred, Beau tried again.

"Janie," he said gently. "Sweetheart, do you know me? It is Beaufort. You told me once that you loved me, and I have never stopped loving you. Tenner has brought me here to greet you. Do you remember me?"

Jane stared at him as if processing his words. They were all looking at her, praying for at least a glimmer of recognition for Beau's sake. The man had waited so very long. Then, it came… a flicker of a smile appeared. The smile widened. A hand came up and she reached out, hesitantly touching his face. A second hand came up so that she was touching both of his cheeks, the blue eyes studying him intently. It seemed to go on forever. Then, she spoke, in a soft and distant voice.

"Beau?" she whispered.

A grin spread across his face as tears filled his eyes. "Aye," he said hoarsely. "It is Beau."

Lady Jane blinked, slowly processing what she'd been told, before moving away from Maude and right into Beau's arms. As he wrapped her up in his big embrace, she collapsed into him, holding him fiercely.

"Beau," she murmured again. "*My* Beau."

"Aye, my sweet," Beau said, struggling not to weep. "I am your Beau. I always will be your Beau, until the end of all things."

She held him ever so tightly, her eyes closed. "I… have missed you."

"I have missed you, too."

For those who had known Lady Jane and Beau before her head injury, there wasn't a dry eye among them. Maude had tears streaming down her face, quickly wiping them away, as Tenner and Arlo looked upon the tender reunion with moist eyes. Even Annalyla, who hadn't known them before, was fighting off tears as she watched a couple who had once loved each other deeply. It was clear that the love was still there.

The entire chamber was filled with it.

"Beau," Annalyla whispered tightly. "Take her into my solar down the hall. You have waited a very long time for this moment and you do not need an audience."

Beau simply nodded, gently turning Jane around and, with his arms around, escorted her from the chamber. Jane seemed very calm and content, nothing like the wild woman Annalyla had first become acquainted with. In Beau's arms, she was where she belonged and no matter how badly her mind was damaged, somewhere deep inside, she knew that this was where she was meant to be.

She finally had her Beaufort.

When they were gone, Maude wiped away the remainder of her tears as she turned to Tenner.

"That was a wonderful thing you did," she said. "I have always said you are a man of great compassion and understanding, Tenner. What you have done for Beau and Jane merely proves it."

Tenner was reluctant to take praise for what, to him, was simply the right thing to do. "You know that their separation has troubled me from the start," he said, looking down at Annalyla, who was gazing up adoringly at him. "Call me foolish and sentimental, but it simply wasn't right for those two to be kept apart any longer. I suppose it was my own happiness that made me realize that. I cannot imagine being kept from Annie, not even if she was no longer the same person. To me, she will always be my Annie, no matter what."

Annalyla smiled at him, putting her soft hand against his cheek. "You and I seem to be in the business of reuniting separated lovers," she said. "First Faustus and Anyu, now Beau and Jane. Everyone has the right to be with the person they love, I think. Everyone deserves to live happily for the rest of their lives."

"I agree."

"How long will Lady Jane be staying with us?"

Tenner kissed the palm of her hand that was still on his face. "Ivor did not make any demands to have her returned soon, so I will keep her here as long as Beau wants me to."

"And if Beau wants to marry her?" Maude asked the question they were, perhaps, all thinking. "He was betrothed to her, once. That love has never died, Ten. What if he wants to marry her?"

Tenner shrugged. "Then he can do it with my blessing," he said. "I'll not stop him. I will even be the one to tell Ivor. All that man wanted to do was keep Jane caged like an animal, so if Beau wants to marry her and take care of her for the rest of her life, then I can think of no more noble destiny for a man."

There was the secret romantic again, the man who had become unbearably sentimental and sweet at times since his marriage to Annalyla. She brought out a side in him that he'd been fearful to expose until she came along. He was no longer rigid in his beliefs, either, but was truly more open and understanding. He was also unafraid to show his emotion.

His wife liked him that way.

"Speaking of destinies," she said after a moment, putting her hand on her belly. "Ours shall soon be here. I am eager for our son to learn from his father, not only the skills of a knight, but the skills of a man. True men do allow themselves to feel and they understand the meaning of love. Beau and Jane are very fortunate to have a friend such as you."

Tenner gave her a lopsided smile, kissing her again as Maude and Arlo excused themselves, leaving the future parents some time alone. Such time was precious, and given Annalyla and Tenner hadn't seen each other in five days, they appreciated the privacy.

They would lose it soon enough.

Two days later, during the midst of a brilliant storm that had rolled in from the sea, Annalyla gave birth to a lusty baby boy, who screamed unhappily in his father's arms as the man wept joyfully all over him.

Little Blaize de Velt looked nothing like the de Velt side of the family. He was born blonde, a distinct de Lohr trait, until his eye color started to develop and it was clear the lad would have the brown eyes with the splash of green in right iris, only in Blaize's case, it was barely noticeable. It gave the child a distinct look, one that Tenner was very proud of. Though a trait he was once embarrassed of, now it defined the de Velt line. He saw it from a different perspective and he was proud of it. There was no mistaking his son, with de Velt and de Lohr blood running through his veins, would also know a great future as his forefathers had.

In time, Blaize was joined by playmates bearing the surnames of de Correa and even de Fira, a trio of lads with the weight of England resting upon their young shoulders, charging forth to find their own great and noble destinies. They had all been born at a castle that, not so long ago, had harbored a dark and terrible reputation. Now, it was a place with a great legacy, with more than one love story for the ages.

Baiadepaura Castle, that desolate fortress on the storm-battered cliffs of Cornwall, had finally found peace.

☙ THE END ❧

Children of Tenner and Annalyla

Blaize

Laurent

Josette

Maxim

Reine

About Kathryn Le Veque

Medieval Just Got Real.

KATHRYN LE VEQUE is a USA TODAY Bestselling author, an Amazon All-Star author, and a #1 bestselling, award-winning, multi-published author in Medieval Historical Romance and Historical Fiction. She has been featured in the NEW YORK TIMES and on USA TODAY's HEA blog. In March 2015, Kathryn was the featured cover story for the March issue of InD'Tale Magazine, the premier Indie author magazine. She was also a quadruple nominee (a record!) for the prestigious RONE awards for 2015.

Kathryn's Medieval Romance novels have been called 'detailed', 'highly romantic', and 'character-rich'. She crafts great adventures of love, battles, passion, and romance in the High Middle Ages. More than that, she writes for both women AND men – an unusual crossover for a romance author – and Kathryn has many male readers who enjoy her stories because of the male perspective, the action, and the adventure.

On October 29, 2015, Amazon launched Kathryn's Kindle Worlds Fan Fiction site WORLD OF DE WOLFE PACK. Please visit Kindle Worlds for Kathryn Le Veque's World of de Wolfe Pack and find many action-packed adventures written by some of the top authors in their genre using Kathryn's characters from the de Wolfe Pack series. As Kindle World's FIRST Historical Romance fan fiction world, Kathryn Le Veque's World of de Wolfe Pack will contain all of the great story-telling you have come to expect.

Kathryn loves to hear from her readers. Please find Kathryn on Facebook at Kathryn Le Veque, Author, or join her on Twitter @kathrynleveque, and don't forget to visit her website and sign up for her blog at www.kathrynleveque.com.

Please follow Kathryn on Bookbub for the latest releases and sales: bookbub.com/authors/kathryn-le-veque.

Made in the USA
Columbia, SC
14 July 2020

13816048R10117